CORNELL WOOLRICH

His name represents steamy, suspenseful mystery fiction. Author of more than 100 stories, novelettes, and books—many dramatized on such classic radio shows as *Climax* and *Suspense* and, on TV, *Alfred Hitchcock Presents*, as well as in feature films—Woolrich is in a class by himself.

CORNELL WOOLRICH

"He has, of course, the photographic eye. He also has a vitality of word and phrase . . . ingenuity and perception and humor."

Dorothy B. Hughes

CORNELL WOOLRICH

"ONE OF THE GREATEST SUSPENSE WRITERS IN THE HISTORY OF CRIME FICTION . . . A LITERARY ARTIST . . . THE EDGAR ALLAN POE OF THE 20th CENTURY."

Francis M. Nevins, Jr.

CORNELL WOOLRICH

One of the truly great and truly original American writers . . . now coming back to readers everywhere from Ballantine Books.

Also by Cornell Woolrich
Published by Ballantine Books:

THE BLACK CURTAIN

The Black Path of Fear

BALLANTINE BOOKS • NEW YORK

 Published in the United States by
Ballantine Books, a division of Random House, Inc., New York,
and simultaneously in Canada by Random House of Canada,
Limited, Toronto, Canada.

ISBN 0-345-30488-8

Manufactured in the United States of America

First Ballantine Books Edition: August 1982

INTRODUCTION

by Francis M. Nevins, Jr.

HE WAS THE POE of the twentieth century and the poet of its shadows. For almost thirty-five years this tormented recluse wrote dozens of haunting suspense stories, the most powerful of their kind ever written—stories full of fear, guilt, and loneliness, breakdown and despair, and a sense that the world is controlled by malignant forces preying on us. And throughout his life he felt those forces eating away at him.

Cornell George Hopley-Woolrich was born in New York City on December 4, 1903, to parents whose marriage collapsed in his youth. Much of his childhood was spent in Mexico with his father, a civil engineer. The experience of seeing Puccini's *Madame Butterfly* in Mexico City at the age of eight gave him his first insight into color and drama, and his first sense of tragedy. Three years later, he understood that someday he too, like Cio-Cio-San, would have to die, and from that moment on he was haunted by a sense of doom that never left him.

During adolescence he returned to Manhattan and lived with his mother and her socially prominent family, and in 1921 he enrolled in Columbia College, with his father paying the tuition from Mexico City. He began writing fiction during an illness in his junior year, and quit school soon afterward to pursue his dream of becoming another F. Scott Fitzgerald. His first novel, *Cover Charge* (1926), chronicles the lives and loves of the Jazz Age's gilded youth in the manner of his current literary idol. This debut was followed by *Children of the Ritz* (1927), a frothy concoction about a spoiled heiress's marriage to her chauffeur, which won him a $10,000 prize contest and a contract from First National Pictures for the movie rights. Woolrich was invited to Hollywood to help with the adaptation and stayed on as a staff writer. Besides his movie chores and an occasional story or article for magazines like *College Humor* and *Smart Set*, he completed three more novels during these years. In December of 1930 he entered a brief and inexplicable marriage with a producer's daughter—inexplicable because for several years he had been homosexual. He continued his secret life after the marriage, prowling the waterfront at night in search of partners, and after the inevitable breakup Woolrich fled back to Manhattan and his mother. The two of them traveled extensively abroad together during the early 1930s. His only novel of the period, *Manhattan Love Song* (1932), anticipates the motifs of his later suspense fiction with its tale of a love-struck young couple cursed by a malignant fate that leaves one dead and the other desolate. But over the next two years he sold almost nothing and was soon deep in debt, reduced to sneaking into movie houses by the fire doors for his entertainment.

In 1934 Woolrich decided to abandon the "literary" world and concentrate on mystery-suspense fiction. He sold three stories to pulp magazines that year, ten more in 1935, and was soon an established professional whose name was a fixture on the covers of *Black Mask, Detective Fiction Weekly, Dime Detective,* and countless other pulps. For the next quarter-century he lived with his mother in a succession of residential hotels, going out only when it was absolutely essential, trapped in a bizarre love–hate relationship that dominated his external world just as the tortured patterns of the inner world of his fiction reflect the strangler grip in which his mother held him.

The more than 100 stories and novelettes Woolrich sold to the pulps before the end of the thirties are richly varied in type, including quasi-police procedurals, rapid-action whizbangs, and encounters with the occult. But the best and the best known of them are the tales of pure edge-of-the-seat suspense, and even their titles reflect the bleakness and despair of their themes: "I Wouldn't Be in Your

Shoes," "Speak to Me of Death," "All at Once, No Alice," "Dusk to Dawn," "Men Must Die," "If I Should Die Before I Wake," "The Living Lie Down with the Dead," "Charlie Won't Be Home Tonight," "You'll Never See Me Again." These and dozens of other Woolrich suspense stories evoke with awesome power the desperation of those who walk the city's darkened streets and the terror that lurks at noonday in commonplace settings. In his hands even such clichéd storylines as the race to save the innocent man from the electric chair and the amnesiac searching for his lost self resonate with human anguish. Woolrich's world is a feverish place where the prevailing emotions are loneliness and fear and the prevailing action a race against time and death. His most characteristic detective stories end with the discovery that no rational account of events is possible, and his suspense stories tend to close not with the dissipation of the terror but with its omnipresence.

The typical Woolrich settings are the seedy hotel, the cheap dance hall, the rundown movie house, and the precinct station backroom. The dominant reality in his world, at least during the thirties, is the Depression, and Woolrich has no peers when it comes to putting us inside the life of a frightened little guy in a tiny apartment with no money, no job, a hungry wife and children, and anxiety consuming him like a cancer. If a Woolrich protagonist is in love, the beloved is likely to vanish in such a way that the protagonist not only can't find her but can't convince anyone that she ever existed. Or, in another classic Woolrich situation, the protagonist comes to after a blackout (caused by amnesia, drugs, hypnosis, or whatever) and little by little becomes convinced that he has committed a murder or other crime while out of himself. The police are rarely sympathetic, for they are the earthly counterparts of the malignant powers that delight in savaging us, and their primary function is to torment the helpless. All we can do about this nightmare world is to create, if we can, a few islands of love and trust to help us forget. But love dies while the lovers go on living, and Woolrich is a master at portraying the corrosion of a relationship between two people. Although he often wrote about the horrors both love and lovelessness can inspire, there are few irredeemably evil characters in his stories, for if one loves or needs love, or is at the brink of destruction, Woolrich identifies with that person no matter what crimes he or she might also have committed. Technically, many of his stories are awful, but like the playwrights of the Absurd, Woolrich uses a senseless tale to hold the mirror to a senseless universe. Some of his tales, indeed, end quite happily (usually thanks to outlandish coincidence), but there are no series characters in his work, and the reader can never know in advance whether a particular story will be light or dark, whether a particular protagonist will end triumphant or dismembered. This is one of the reasons that his stories are so hauntingly suspenseful.

So much for the motifs, beliefs, and devices at the core of Woolrich's fiction. In 1940 he joined the migration of pulp mystery writers from lurid-covered magazines to hardcover books, and with his first suspense novel, *The Bride Wore Black* (1940), he launched his so-called Black Series, which influenced the French *roman noir* and the development of the bleak Hollywood crime movies of the forties, which the French have labeled *film noir*. Julie Killeen, whose husband was killed on the church steps moments after their marriage, spends years tracking down and systematically murdering the drunk driver and his four cronies whom she holds responsible for the beloved's death. Eventually she is herself stalked through the years by homicide cop Lew Wanger, and when their paths finally converge both hunters find themselves in the presence of the malignant powers.

The second novel in the cycle was *The Black Curtain* (1941), the masterpiece on the overworked subject of amnesia. Frank Townsend recovers from a three years' loss of memory, becomes obsessed with the determination to learn who and what he was during those missing years, and finds love, hate, and a murder charge waiting for him behind the curtain. *Black Alibi* (1942) is a terror novel about a killer jaguar menacing a large South American city, while a lone Anglo hunts a human murderer who may be hiding behind the jaguar's claws. *The Black Angel* (1943) deals with a terrified young wife's race against time to prove that her convicted husband did not murder his girl friend and that some other man in the dead woman's life is guilty. *The Black Path of Fear* (1944), which you are about to read, tells of a man who runs away to Havana with an American gangster's wife, followed by the vengeful husband, who kills the woman and frames her lover, leaving him a stranger in a strange land, menaced on all sides and fighting for his life. And the final novel in the series, *Rendezvous in Black* (1948), is a creative reworking of the avenging angel motif from *The Bride Wore Black* but with the sexes reversed: A grief-crazed young man, holding one among a small group of people responsible for his fiancée's death, devotes his life to entering the lives of each of that group in turn, finding out whom each one most loves, and murdering these loved ones so that the person who killed his fiancée will live the grief he lives.

Like most of Woolrich's novels, *The Black Path of Fear* was based on one of his stories for the pulps (in this case "Havana Night," in *Flynn's Detective Magazine,* formerly *Detective Fiction Weekly,* for December 1942). The dope dens and sinister Orientals and secret passages and hair's-breadth escapes, which he added to the earlier story to make it book length, don't represent Woolrich at his best, exciting and action-crammed though these pages are. But the earlier chapters with their evocations of love discovered and love destroyed, their sense of what it must be like to be alone and hunted through a nightmare city of the mind, furnish reason after reason for the view that Woolrich was the greatest suspense writer that ever lived.

Other media quickly introduced the book to a wider audience. CBS Radio's classic series *Suspense* aired a superb thirty-minute version on August 31, 1944, with Brian Donlevy as Scott, and repeated the same adaptation March 7, 1946, with the even better Cary Grant in the lead. Later in 1946 United Artists released a full-length film version, *The Chase,* directed by the erratic Arthur Ripley from a script by Philip Yordan, and starring Robert Cummings, Michele Morgan, Steve Cochran, and Peter Lorre. It was a bizarre picture, infamous among Woolrichphiles for the way Ripley and Yordan scuttled the novel's bleak vision by having all the nightmare events turn out to be just that—a bad dream from which the protagonist awakes! The movie was later adapted into a sixty-minute radio play (*This Is Hollywood,* November 9, 1946) with Robert Montgomery and Michele Morgan, and several years later into a live sixty-minute TV drama (*Lux Video Theater,* December 30, 1954), starring Ruth Roman, Pat O'Brien, and a pre-*Gunsmoke* James Arness. From the brief descriptions available, these versions apparently had even less relation to Woolrich's novel than did the movie.

During the early 1940s Woolrich continued to write stories and novelettes for the pulps, and dozens of his huge backlog of earlier stories were adapted for dramatic radio on series like *Suspense* and *Molle Mystery Theatre.* As the novels increased his reputation, publishers issued numerous hardcover and paperback collections of his shorter tales, and many of his books and stories were made into *films noir* of the forties (although the most famous Woolrich-based film, Alfred Hitchcock's *Rear Window,* was made in 1954). As if all this activity were not enough, Woolrich continued to write more novels, too many for publication under a single byline, so that he adopted the pseudonyms of William Irish and (his own two middle names) George Hopley for some of his most suspenseful books.

The Irish byline debuted in *Phantom Lady* (1942), in which an innocent man is sentenced to die for the murder of his wife, while his two best friends race the clock to find the apparently nonexistent woman who can give the husband an alibi. The second Irish, *Deadline at Dawn* (1944), is another clock-race story, with a desperate young couple given until sunrise to clear themselves of a murder charge and escape the web of the city. In *Night Has a Thousand Eyes* (1945), as by Hopley, the suspense rises to unbearable pitch as a simple-minded recluse with uncanny powers predicts a millionaire's imminent death by the jaws of a lion, and the doomed man's daughter and a sympathetic cop struggle to avert a destiny that they suspect, and soon come to hope, was conceived by a merely human power. *Waltz into Darkness* (1947), also written as Irish, is set in New Orleans around 1880 and tells of the hopeless love affair between an unbearably lonely man and an impossibly evil woman. And in the last Irish novel of the forties, *I Married a Dead Man* (1948), a woman with nothing to live for, fleeing from her sadistic husband, is injured in a train wreck, is mistaken for another woman with everything to live for who was killed in the crackup, grasps this heaven-sent chance to start life over with a new identity, falls in love again, and is destroyed by malignant powers along with the man she loves.

Despite overwhelming financial and critical success, Woolrich's personal situation remained as wretched as ever. His mother's prolonged illnesses seemed to paralyze his ability to write, and after 1948 he published very little: one minor novel under each of his three bylines in 1950–51, and a few short stories. That he was remembered at all during the fifties is largely due to Ellery Queen (Frederic Dannay), who reprinted a quantity of Woolrich's pulp tales in *Ellery Queen's Mystery Magazine.* But Woolrich and his mother continued to live in comfortable isolation, for his magazine tales proved to be as adaptable to television as they had been to radio a decade earlier, and series like *Ford Theater, Alfred Hitchcock Presents,* and *Schlitz Playhouse of Stars* frequently presented thirty-minute filmed versions of his stories. Indeed even the prestigious *Playhouse 90* made use of Woolrich, turning *Rendezvous in Black* into a feature-length teledrama (broadcast October 25, 1956), starring Franchot Tone, Laraine Day, and Boris Karloff.

When his mother died, in 1957, Woolrich cracked. Diabetic, alcoholic, wracked by self-contempt, and alone, he dragged out the last years of his life. He continued to write but left unfinished much more than he ever completed, and the only new work that saw print in his last years was a handful of final "tales of love and despair." He developed gangrene in his leg and let it go untended for so long that when he finally sought medical help the doctor had no choice but to amputate. After the operation he lived in a wheelchair, unable to learn how to walk on an artificial leg. On September 25, 1968, he died of a stroke, leaving unfinished two novels, a collection of short stories, and an autobiography. He had prepared a long list of titles for stories he'd never even begun, and one of these captures his bleak world view in a single phrase: "First You Dream, Then You Die." He left no survivors, and only a tiny handful of people attended his funeral. His estate of nearly a million dollars was bequeathed in trust to Columbia University, where his literary career had begun, to establish a scholarship fund for students of creative writing. The fund is named for Woolrich's mother.

"I was only trying to cheat death," he wrote in a fragment found among his papers. "I was only trying to surmount for a little while the darkness that all my life I surely knew was going to come rolling in on me some day and obliterate me. I was only trying to stay alive a little brief while longer, after I was already gone." Trapped in a wretched psychological environment and gifted, or cursed, with an understanding of his own and everyone's trappedness, he shaped his solitude into stories that will haunt our descendants as they haunted our forebears. He could not escape death, but the world he imagined, will.

CHAPTER I

SOMEHOW WE'D GOTTEN INTO Zulueta Street. Maybe the driver figured we'd wind up there eventually anyhow. Everyone seems to. We dawdled up to Sloppy Joe's, all open to the street, and looking better before you go in than it does inside.

The horse seemed to stop of its own accord. I guess it had been here so many times before it knew the place. The coachman turned his head around and looked at us inquiringly.

"What's this?" I said.

"Esloppy's," he said, "Big *attracción.*"

I felt like saying, "What are you, their steerer or something?" I didn't bother.

I turned and looked at her. "You want to?"

She didn't want to go in at first. "Do you think it's safe for us to show ourselves around like this, Scott?"

"Sure it's safe. This is Havana, not the States any more. He hasn't got that long a reach."

She smiled at me. One of those smiles of hers that—oh, brother, you feel like the soft end of the sealing wax going onto an envelope flap. "Hasn't he?" she said. "We should have gone to a hotel and locked ourselves in."

I thought to myself: You bet we should, and thrown the key away. But not on his account.

I said: "But he sent you a radiogram wishing you luck."

"That's why I'm worried," she said. "He didn't say which kind of luck."

"I'm with you," I said.

She smiled again. I felt like used-up chewing gum, only not so sturdy. "And I'm with you," she said. "And we can only die once."

I handed her down. She stood there for a minute and she lighted the whole street up, like a torch. I was surprised there weren't reflections on the dim walls around us. She was all in white, to fit the climate and the night; satin, I think it was, and I think, too, it must have been sprayed on and then allowed to dry, to be that even all over. She had on everything he'd ever given her, and there were rippling flashes at her ears and throat and wrists and fingers every time she moved.

I wondered why she'd put it all on and brought it ashore with her like this, especially after the way she'd told me she felt about it only the other night. "They *talk* to me sometimes at night, Scotty. I lie awake in the dark and I can hear them. Piece by piece, from the dresser top, in funny squeaky little voices, each one in turn. 'Remember when you got *me?* Remember *that?*' And 'Remember what *I* cost you? Surely you remember *that?*' Until I can't stand it any more. Until I stop up my ears and think I'll go mad."

I'd asked her about it in the launch coming ashore just now. "I know we're going to do the town, but don't you think you're a little heavy-hung with the rock candy?"

She said, "I didn't think it would be a good idea to leave it around the stateroom while we're standing in the harbor."

"Why didn't you turn it over to the purser?"

She started to unfasten the catch of one of the pieces at her wrist. "I'll drop it in if you say so. All of it. Right now. Every last piece." She wasn't kidding, either. I had to pull her hand back from over the gunwale of the launch.

I don't think she knew herself why she'd put it on. Some sort of defiance, maybe, was at the bottom of it. His jewelry to please another man's eyes.

I paid the coachman and we went in. It was jammed to the sidewalk line, nearly, and the musicians were pounding away up on a screwy little balcony it had tacked up on the wall over everyone's heads. You couldn't see the bar; you could see only an open ditch up front past all their heads that showed where it was.

I went in first and dug a tunnel through for her and

then drew her in after me with a hand at her wrist. We got through to the second layer of customers, then the density held us off for a while. It was like being in a football scrimmage. Then we got a break; I managed to get a grip on the edge of the bar with one hand when someone backed out, and I pulled the two of us into the empty hole there that had only taken one before, and there we were, crushed up tight against one another and not minding at all. I said, "Two dikes."

I didn't even have to hitch my head to kiss her, just change my mouth around a little. Which I did.

I said, "Are you all right?"

She smiled that smile again. She said, "Your arm around me, your shoulder just behind me—oh, let it come, Scotty, let it come."

"Don't keep saying that," I answered, low. I'm funny that way; when I was a kid I used to think that when you said a thing over too many times you brought it on. I guess a little of that is still left over in me.

Her looks were creating a continual swirling ripple round us, sucking all sorts of vendors and steerers through the crowd. They kept buzzing around like bottle flies, all trying to sell something at once, from imported Paris perfume—imported by way of Brooklyn—to a good address with no questions asked and the sort of post cards that you don't send home. We didn't even hear them; we were in a world of our own.

She downed half her drink without taking a breath and smiled that smile again at me. "Let's hope it has time to go to my head."

Someone touched my shoulder, which was as good as touching hers too. Everything you had in that crowd belonged to three or four others as well. We both turned our heads.

A Cuban had struggled through with an old-fashioned tripod. "The señor and lady would like a peek-ture for to show their friends back in Estates?"

"Christ," I said to her deprecatingly.

She picked the idea up. It seemed to appeal to her. Same principle as the diamonds, most likely. "I know someone would love to get one. Why not? Go ahead. Take us like *this*, photographer. Look, like *this*." She wound her arm around my neck and closed it like a nutcracker. She pressed her cheek to mine, pasted our two faces together like that. We stayed like that. "Like *this,*" she said bitterly. "With love!"

"Sh-h," I said gently. I hadn't realized she hated him so until now. I should have, but I hadn't. It made me feel good. It made me feel lucky. It made me feel humble.

I don't know how he got them back, but he got them back a little. I guess they didn't want to get singed. He got a little floor space cleared, about the size of a silver dollar, and poked the three legs of the tripod down into that. Then he covered his head, and those of two other fellows as well, with a black cloth. The other two fellows worked theirs clear again, but he left his underneath. Then he held up his hand straight overhead with a little trowel thing in it. One of the side lines of the place is these flashlight photos they keep banging off all the time all around the bar.

We held it. The flashlight powder fizzed blue and lit up the whole place. I could feel her give a little jolt against me. I gave a little jolt myself, for that matter.

The regular yellow kind of light came right back again. The smell drifted past and then went away.

I hadn't known she weighed that much. I said, "He's taken us now."

She just clung on.

"Ah, come on," I remonstrated gently. "Everybody's looking at us." I could hear them laughing around us. They thought we were lit, I guess, the way she was draped there.

She said faintly, close to my ear: "Don't rush me, Scotty. Give me time." And tried to find my lips with hers.

I joined them up with hers, quick. I said, "What is it? Why're you so limp?"

"I knew we wouldn't make it," she whispered. "What do we care? Part of a night's better than none at all."

I must have opened my grip a little without knowing it. Suddenly she cascaded down the front of me like rippling water and lay in a tumbled heap at my feet. For a second there were just strangers' faces left behind up there, where she had been, staring back at me. Then I dropped down by her to see what was the matter; we were together again. I hadn't gotten it yet. I hadn't caught up. All there were were motionless legs around us, like a knobby picket fence walling us in together. Up in the gallery the five-piece band was giving "Siboney" a loud going-over just then. That's the tune they play everywhere down there, "Siboney." That's the tune that had been following us through the night. It makes a good dirge. It breaks your heart for you.

She even looked pretty down there. The shadow of the overhanging bar cast a soft, peaceful twilight over her. I tried to pick her up in my arms, and she made an indifferent little pass with her hand, as if to tell me there wasn't time.

"Just stay with me a minute. It won't take long."

I got down close and kneaded her to me; I didn't know what other way to try to keep her with me. I didn't know; I didn't know.

"I've got to go out alone in the dark," she sighed, "and I've always hated the dark." Her lips tried to find mine, then they gave up. "Scotty," she breathed, "finish my drink for me. It's still standing up there. And bust the glass. That's the way I want to go. And, Scotty—let me know how that picture you and I took turns out."

Her chin gave a dejected little dip, and I was by myself without her; she'd gone somewhere else.

Hands were reaching down, and I slashed them away. What was left there was mine; they couldn't have it.

I picked her up in my arms, and I staggered to my feet and looked around. I didn't know where to go or what to go there for.

Somebody pointed, and I looked down at the floor under her. Small dark red drops were falling one by one, very sluggish, very slow. You couldn't see them drop; you could only see them after they hit. They made intricate little patterns, like burgundy snowflakes or midget garnet starfish on a beach. There was something sticking out of her side, like an ornamental brooch or clasp to her dress. But it thrust out a little too far; it couldn't have been meant to jack out like that. It was jade, and it was vibrating slightly as I held her. Not with her own breath—there wasn't any more of that—but with the shaking of my own trembling hold upon her.

It looked vaguely familiar. It was carved in the shape of a small, squatting monkey holding paws to his eyes. I couldn't think for a minute where I'd seen it before. I only knew it had no business to be where it was. I tightened my hand around it and pulled at it, and it grew bigger. At my pulling there was more of it and more of it and more of it, like in some horrid nightmare. It was like pulling her apart with my bare hand; pulling her flesh apart, pulling her insides out—I don't know how to say it. The steel part showed up below the monkey and kept coming, kept coming, by eighths of inches. And my sweat kept coming out on my forehead, as though this obstruction were coming out of me. It came slowly free, the rest of it, the stinger, the tail part; steely, straight, graceful and thin and deadly. It was like looking at death to look at it. It *was* death. Suddenly it had finished coming; there wasn't any more. It had ended. And there was just a hole there, where it had been. With blood down inside it, but too lazy to come out any more. Or already too old.

My palm stretched out, under and beyond her body, as if it were asking alms. And in it the monkey. And out beyond that, the long steel thing with her blood upon it. Making a sort of moiré surface.

I opened my fingers spasmodically, and it dropped to the floor with a clash.

I finally got it. Don't laugh; I was slow. When you're in love you're slow like that.

I saw their faces there before me and I wanted help, anywhere I could get it.

"She's dead!" I shouted at them. "She doesn't move! She's been knifed right in my arms!"

My pain was in English. Their fright was in Spanish. There are no different languages for things like that. They're all the same.

I heard the word go up from a dozen different throats at once, and I knew it, though I'd never heard it before.

There was a sudden stampede that nearly burst the flimsy seams of the place. Every man for himself, and the devil take the hindmost. This wasn't for them; this was mine, and I could have her. They went stumbling and floundering all over each other in their hurry to get out into the street and avoid being snagged as witnesses. I suppose that was it mainly. And the chance to skip without paying for their drinks was too good to be missed; that must have been partly it too. And the rest was just sheer panic, catching from one to the other. Panic, which is fear without any real reason to be afraid.

I even saw one of the hindmost miss his footing and go down on hands and knees. Then he picked himself up and went scampering outside after the rest.

I was left alone in there with my dead. Just me and her and a long, long row of abandoned drinks lined up along the bar, all sizes, shapes, and colors. And the men behind the bar who'd had to stay there because they couldn't get out fast enough.

I guess I stood there. I don't think I moved. Dimly I realized there wasn't any use going any other place with her, because she'd be dead in that other place, too, just as dead as here.

It didn't take long. Havana's a fast town for anything: love, and life, and death too.

Then the screech of police cars came careening into the narrow reaches of Zulueta Street, from way up at the far end, and whistled down it and stopped outside. And the uniforms of cops and duck and pongee suits of plain-clothes men came spilling in between the supporting posts that along most of its street front is all Sloppy's has for outside walls. And the brave ones ganged up again now and came in once more, but behind the police and not in front of them. Which makes a good deal of difference when it comes to the detention of witnesses.

They took her from me and stretched her out on three chairs slung together in a row; that was the best the place could provide in the way of a bier. Her skirt had hitched up a little too high on one side, and I gently freed it and paid it down to where it belonged. Gee, that hurt; I don't know why. I turned my back and stepped across to the bar.

While they were milling around her, and their police medical examiner—I suppose he was that—was busy with her, I picked up the daiquiri she'd left standing on the bar. I saluted her with it, not where she was but up a little just over my eyes, and drained it to the bottom. And that hurt too; what a bitter drink. Then I snapped the stem of the glass off short. Good-by. It wasn't much of a funeral service. It was all there was time for just then.

They closed in around me and my afterlife had begun. The new, lonely stretch without her. All by myself in a strange town. Two of them had revolvers out, I noticed vaguely. I wondered why. There wasn't anyone in there that could hurt them or threaten them. I was the only one in there, in the middle of all of them. The rest of the crowd had been pushed back outside again.

They tried saying a couple of things that I couldn't understand. Then when they saw that they called for someone by name. "Acosta," they kept saying and turning their heads. I guess it was a name, anyway. Some new guy stepped through their ranks and took over.

He was in plain clothes: an alpaca suit. He had horn-rimmed glasses and he looked studious. I guess he was one of their ace detectives; there was a sort of overtone of deference all around. He had a good working knowledge of English, the kind that you don't get from books but that gets rubbed into your elbows from knocking around. It was spiced with accent, but his word patterns came out like ours do. He must have been educated up in the States or gone to one of our police schools up there.

He came up close to me and looked me over.

"This woman is dead."

I didn't say anything; my heart was punchy from knowing it.

"You were the man with her?"

"I was the man with her."

"Your name?"

"Scott. Bill Scott." He had a notebook going. "Make it William as long as it's for the blotter."

"Her name?"

That was going to hurt. I shifted my jaw into low. "How do you want it—formal, or the way it really was, or—the way it was going to be?"

You didn't horse around with him. "I want her name. That's a plain enough question. Or isn't it?"

"Eve," I said softly. "Mrs. Eddie Roman on the books. It was going to be—"

That hurt too much; it took half the lining of my throat with it.

"It was going to be?"

"Mrs. Bill Scott," I whispered. "Somebody didn't give us a chance."

"And where is Mr. Roman?"

"Not," I said, "where I'd like him to be. Which is frying in hell."

"Your address in La Habana?"

"Down here where my shoes are standing."

"Hers?"

"Neither of us have any. We got in on the Ward liner that docked at three this afternoon. So if you've got to have an address, put us down for staterooms B-21 and B-23, just across the passage from one another. My razor blades and our toothbrushes are still in there, so I guess that makes it an address."

"Just across the passage from one another."

"Take it easy," I said. "Once was enough on that."

He put the notebook away. I thought that ended it. I was wrong; that only began it. "Now," he said.

"Now what?"

"You had a quarrel with her here in this bar?"

"I had a quarrel with her like hell here in this bar."

He just looked at me. I got it. I was a half lap behind again, like when I'd picked her up from the floor.

"Wait a minute. What was that for, just then? Which way are you heading?"

"Toward facts. Toward the truth."

"Well, you're going the wrong way, then." I kept my voice steady. My throat swelled a little, pressed out against my collar; that was all. "I didn't do it."

Somebody in the official group around set off a string of little Spanish firecrackers: pop, pop, pop, pop. He switched the sound off with a cut of his hand. As if to say, "I know that as well as you, but he's entitled to a hearing." I liked that even less than the original protest.

"Is this your knife?" They'd picked it up long ago.

That jade handle, carved into the shape of a monkey holding its eyes covered, had looked damn familiar from the beginning. I'd placed it by now. I knew I'd better tell them; they were going to find out for themselves in another minute anyway. There was nothing to hide about it after all.

"No," I said. "But it's a very close match. I did buy one just like it this afternoon in a curiosity shop. Wait a minute, I'll show you. I've got it in my pocket right—"

They caught the half start my hand made toward the inside pocket of my coat, grabbed me in about three different places: my shoulder, my elbow, and my wrist. Also on the opposite arm, in about three more.

"Wait a minute, don't get so excited," I said in cold reproof. "What do you think I'm going to do?"

"We don't know," he told me. "But whatever **it is**, we'll do it for you."

"What're you trying to do—make a suspect out of me, searching me like this?"

He gave me a lesson in grammar. "You don't make something out of a thing when it's that already."

I made a sandwich of that between two lumps and swallowed it.

They went over me thoroughly. I kept waiting for them to get to it, to bring it out, so they could see it wasn't the same one. When they had finished the knife didn't come out, just the receipt for it.

I squirmed around in their clutches while they were scanning it. "Wait a minute, there's a knife in there that goes with that!" I kept writhing, trying to get up and into that particular pocket myself. There was too much dead weight anchoring my arms.

Finally one of them pulled the lining up to show me. It came up empty.

"But there was a knife in there!"

Acosta tapped it palmwise a couple of times. "There *was* a knife in there. And this is it!"

I kept my voice steady, low. This would be straightened out in a minute. No use getting excited; that would only hinder my being able to make them understand.

"Now look, just listen to me a minute. That couldn't be the one. I didn't take mine out. It was still wrapped, the way he gave it to me. I'll tell you just how too. In—in green oiled paper, held down with two rubber bands, one at each end."

He jerked his thumb at the two holding onto me, and they swiveled me aside out of the way. The way you roll something standing on a truncated base. He crouched down into that twilight she'd died in at the foot of the bar. He pawed three times, here, there, over in the next place, came up with a crumpled ball of green oiled paper and two rubber bands in his palm.

"Very accurate." He nodded.

I pitched my chin upward at him. "Are you trying to tell me I stood there in the middle of that crowd, deliberately took that knife out of my pocket, stripped the paper and the rubber bands off it, and drove it into her—without being seen?"

"Are you trying to tell us somebody else did that, without your feeling, seeing, or hearing him? Listen how this stuff crackles." He gave the paper wad a crunch, and it sputtered and hissed in the middle of his hand like something alive.

He waited a minute for that to sink in. Then he gave me an unwarm smile. It didn't mean "Let's be buddies."

"Do you still deny this is your knife?"

I kept staring at the damn thing, half scared of it now myself. It was bewitched or something. How could it get out of there, where I'd had it, and into her?

He took the receipt from the man holding it, translated it aloud for my benefit, word for word. It wasn't one of those shorthand things you get up North. It was written out in great detail; it was a young book. It was in flowery Spanish. When I'd seen him composing it back there where I'd bought it, I'd thought that was the custom down there, to write out a complete description of each purchase, practically give its life history.

" 'The Curiosity and Novelty Shop of Tío Chin,' " Acosta read off, " '42, Pasaje Angosta. For the sale of one ornamental knife, imported oriental, jade grip, to the Mister Scott—' "

Maybe his reading it out like that brought the scene back. A light suddenly dawned on me. I saw what it was that had been bothering me all along. It was going to be all right now. The worst was over. "Wait," I interrupted him breathlessly. "Let me see that knife; let me see it closer. Just hold the handle up so I can get a good look at it. It's a pretty small carving."

He held it up sort of ironically, pinched between two fingers at the neck.

"It's holding its eyes covered, the little monkey. Right?"

"We see that too," he said dryly.

"Well, that isn't the one I bought."

I waited triumphantly for that to sink it. If it did, you couldn't tell.

"He had a set of three there—eyes, ears, and mouth. You know, illustrating the old proverb or whatever it is, 'See no evil, hear no evil, speak no evil.' I didn't want all three. I asked her which I should pick, and she suggested the one holding its ears. And that's the one I took. This is a mate to it, but it's not the same knife. This is somebody else's knife. *He*'ll tell you, the old guy where I bought it. Let's go back there; I can prove it by him."

They didn't stir.

Acosta changed back to the receipt again. "Do you deny that this bill of sale was made out to you?"

That was dumb. They'd taken it right out of my own pocket, hadn't they? "No, of course not. That's my receipt, all right."

"Then suppose you let me finish reading it to you. You didn't give me time." He went on: " 'Description—with handle carving of the monkey that sees no evil. Received payment, twenty pesos.' "

My jaw hung slack while that sank in. "No. He got it wrong on the receipt, that's all!"

It was no good. "You have admitted you bought a knife. You have admitted this is the receipt for the knife you bought. There is the knife she was killed with in front of you. You admit that is the one, since it was projecting from her; you yourself withdrew it? All that is necessary, then, is for the three things to fit one another. Here is the receipt, from your own pocket, with your own name on it, that fits the knife she was killed with—'the monkey that sees no evil.' The receipt fits the knife; the knife fits the wound. Therefore, the wound fits the receipt, and the receipt is made out to you." He gave a shrug. "It's simple. A complete circle without any opening."

If it was, I went hopping around on the inside of it, trying to get out. "But I tell you I bought the knife of the monkey that *hears* no evil! This is somebody else's knife! *This* knife fits the wound, and the receipt fits *this* knife, all right. But the receipt *doesn't* fit the knife I bought. That's a different knife! Can't you get that through your heads?"

"Anglo-Saxon indirection," he told me patronizingly. "You people always take the longest way around between two points. Just like you tangle up centimeters into fractions of inches." He was going to convince me. He not only liked to arrest people; he liked to convert them to a sense of their guilt as well. He was going to show me what a tough spot I was in. I didn't know. I was just passing time chinning with them in a bar because I didn't have anything better to do.

"Suppose for the sake of argument we say it is somebody else's knife—although it isn't." He spread his hands. "Then there is still one missing. Where is the one you say you bought? Where is the one you even told us how it was wrapped for you—in green paper, rubber bands? Where is the one you say you had in your pocket, that you stood there so surprised we didn't take it out? Well? Where? You say there are two. It isn't we who say there are two. We say there is one. We show you the one. You say there are two. But you can't show us the two. Well, who is wrong—you or we?"

I was going slowly nuts. "It might have fallen out of my pocket in the carriage, in the place we ate, anywhere. We dined at Sans Souci and even got up a couple of times to rumba. It might have been then. How do I know? The pocket wasn't deep enough to hold it—it overhung the lining—I saw that when I first stuffed it in."

This brought on a burst of laughter when he had translated it for the benefit of the rest. One of them pinched the end of his nose tight, which means the same thing in any language.

Acosta addressed himself to me again. "It unwrapped itself first and then fell out. Skinned itself like a snake does, leaving the green paper and rubber bands behind in your pocket until you got here! Then *they* fell out by themselves. And meanwhile, of course, the receipt was for a different knife the whole time. That's what storekeepers give out receipts for, to show which article you *didn't* buy, and not which article you *did* buy."

I tried to stop him, but he went right ahead. No Marquess of Queensberry rules in this kind of clinch.

"So the receipt was for a different knife. Then this *different* knife mysteriously shows up right here, out of all La Habana, at your feet in Sloppy Joe's barroom, to catch up with its own receipt. It followed you around like a filing to a magnet, maybe, eh? You take the receipt out of the store first, and then the knife it belongs to gets up and floats out after you, drops here, *ping!* to the floor at your feet, after first sticking itself into the lady." He made a windmill sweep of his arms. "Is this the kind of story you expect us to swallow? You think because you are in Cuba you can talk to us like a bunch of six-year-old kids? What kind of police you think we are down here, anyway?"

I said limply: "I'm all tangled up now. But here's what I'm trying to get at. If I *was* going to kill her, why would I come into a crowded place like this to do it? We were alone in a carriage, driving along the sea wall in the dark, just before we came in here. One time we even stopped and sat there, looking at the harbor, and the driver got down and strolled off to stretch his legs. Why didn't I do it there? Why didn't I do it then?"

He had one for that too. And quick, without a hitch. "Because a crowd gives you more cover. The bigger the crowd, the bigger the cover-up. If you did it while you were alone with her, there could be no mistaking who did it. You and nobody else. Here, with people thick around you, you had a better chance to pass it off as somebody else's doing. Like you are trying to."

"But it *was* somebody else's doing!" I clawed at my collar to get it out of the way, but my hand couldn't make it, it still had too much tonnage fastened to it.

"I will show you why it couldn't be." He hadn't had so much fun since his last promotion, I bet. "You will prove it for me out of your own mouth by answering three questions." He matched three fingers to them. "How long had this woman been in La Habana?"

I'd already told them once. What was the good of going back on that now? "She got off the boat with me a little before six this evening."

One finger went down. "Four hours ago!" He crowded in on me closer. "Had she ever been here before?"

I had to tell him the truth on that too; it would have been easy enough to find out later. "Neither of us ever had."

The second finger went down. He had my kidneys pinned against the bar by now. "Did she know anyone here? Anyone at all, even at second hand, even by letter of introduction?"

The truth seemed to keep working against me. "No," I

admitted in an undertone. "Not a soul. No one at all." That was why we'd come here.

The third finger went down. He was supposed to have me inside the fist that was left. Maybe he did, at that. "There's your answer. Do you still want to claim somebody else but you killed her, in a place where she had just arrived, in a place where she knew no one, in a place where she had never been in her life before? Above all, *with your own knife,* taken out of your pocket and unwrapped before being used!"

There comes that knife again, I thought dismally.

They were ready to take her out now. I saw them taking off her rings and bracelets and things. I don't know why they were doing it here instead of at the morgue or wherever it was they were taking her. Maybe they figured there's too many a slip, even on your last ride, and she just might show up there without them.

All the shine, all the glitter waned and went out at her throat and ears and wrists and fingers. She was going to send them all back to him anyway, I thought. She didn't want them. They'd cost her too much. More than he'd ever paid over any jewelry counter for them. They used to speak to her at nights from the top of the dresser and keep her awake, she told me. And even when she crammed them into a box and stuffed them away, to shut them up, she could still hear their faint whispers coming through. That was after she'd met me, when what she'd done with herself first counted. She hadn't wanted them; she was going to get rid of them. But now they were here. And she wasn't any more. Just that deflated white dress over there on those three chairs, so flat, so straight, so still.

Even her perfume was still here. But she wasn't. Everything had lasted longer than she had. Even my poor, clumsy love.

They dumped them all together into a large handkerchief and tied the four corners up and tossed it across the room to Acosta, like a beanbag, for safekeeping.

Then they picked her up and started her on that long last trip she had to take alone. I tried to go with her at least as far as the morgue truck they had backed up outside, but they wouldn't let me; they held me fast there. She'd never liked the dark; I remember her telling me that many times. She'd never liked to be alone in it, either. And now she had to go there, where that was all there was, just those two things. I stood there, very still and very straight, with my eyes on her to the last.

So she went out that way, into the black Havana night, without diamonds, without love, without dreams.

I don't know how many minutes went by after that. They seemed like a lot, but maybe they were few; they hit me so slow and empty. Then somebody said something to me; I didn't hear what it was.

"Let me alone, will you?" I answered dully. "I don't know whether I'm coming or I'm going."

"You're coming," Acosta answered. "You're coming with us." A hand that weighed a ton clamped itself onto my shoulder. "*¡Adelante!*" Meaning, start moving. "You are under arrest for murder."

CHAPTER II

THE CHINESE SECTION OF Havana makes up in noise and overcrowdedness for what it lacks in size. It makes the Chinatowns of our cities up North look like lifeless ghost towns by comparison, and some of them aren't slouches when it comes to being thickly peopled. But this was a veritable anthill of swarming humanity; I'd never seen anything like it. The police car, with me in the back seat between Acosta and one of the other department men, had to crawl along at a snail's pace through the crooked, teeming streets. It would have been quicker to walk it, but maybe they felt that the car, with its official license plates and one of the men riding supercargo on the running boards, added prestige. It was certainly no help. The man at the wheel drove with one hand, his other tapping the signal button like a telegraph key. I don't think we covered a soundless yard along the way. The continual blats coming from us only added to the din all around us. It was enough to wreck your nerves in short order—that is, if you still cared whether they were wrecked or not. I didn't, so I wasn't affected by it.

Where the way was wide enough they could get out of our way by flattening themselves against the walls on either side of us. But plenty of the time even that wouldn't do it; they had to get in altogether, back up into doorways, until we'd passed by. And when they were street peddlers—and enough of them were—and had a lot of truck piled up on their heads, even that wouldn't do it; they had to hoist themselves up on something and let us glide by below. And the man on that side of the seat had to lower his head. Several times like that we cruised by beneath momentary umbrellas of fly-active sweets or pyramided panama hats held agonizedly aloft over us. It was a peculiar way to be taken anywhere under arrest, to say the least.

This, I kept reminding myself, was supposed to be my last chance to clear myself. They were giving me this last chance, unasked. Or, rather, I had mentioned it once earlier back there at the bar, but by now it was strictly their own idea, not mine; I didn't much care any more. What they were out for was verbal substantiation, from the Chinaman from whom I'd bought the knife, that I'd actually left there with the hear-no-evil one, that that was the one he'd wrapped for me, that he'd absent-mindedly made out the wrong receipt. Even that wouldn't be enough to clear me altogether any more; I was in too deep by now. But at least it would make the odds more even. By supporting this one feature of my story it would indirectly strengthen all the rest of it at the same time. Any story is always as strong as its weakest detail. This detail mayn't have been the weakest one, but at least it was the most easily proven. In fact, it was the only one that I could get a witness for. The rest was just my own unsupported word.

I wasn't much worried about getting his corroboration; I knew I could count on it, but the strange part of it was I didn't particularly care by this time one way or the other. These guys in the car with me were looking at it from the police point of view; I was looking at it from my own personal point of view.

She was gone, so what difference did all the rest of it make? The hell with the rest of it. I just sat there staring woodenly ahead. They could get there fast or they could get there slow or they could get there never; to me it was all the same.

We hit this Pasaje Angosta finally and sealed it up by stopping lengthwise across it. At that it only reached from windshield to the hinges on the rear door; the rest of the car was all overlap. If I'd thought the streets before this were narrow, they were parade grounds compared to this. It was more like a slit inadvertently left when two buildings are put side by side and don't quite come together. We had to stop the way we did, broadside; to have tried to turn the car and wedge it in there would have either shorn the hub-caps and the fenders off or gouged the plaster and fill out of the walls on each side.

As though we weren't jammed up enough, already, right away, as soon as we became static, the place started to choke up around us with onlookers. And there's nothing so passively immovable as a Chinese crowd.

Acosta got down and peered into the chasm facing us. "This is it, isn't it, Escott?" he said briskly.

I turned my head. I'd still been looking forward until now. "This is it."

He hitched his elbow at me, and I got down and stood next to him. Then the other guy got down in back of me. They both took a grip on me, and they led me forward and into it, very much the prisoner, with one of them making a tourniquet of the slack of my coat collar and the other one making one of the back of my sleeve. At that we couldn't go three abreast; we went sort of on the bias, with me the middle link. The others stayed with the car.

It fooled you. It kept going and kept going. It even got a little wider than it had been at its mouth; not much, but just a little. It smelled; boy, how it smelled. Like asafetida, and somebody burning feathers, and the lee side of a sewer. It wasn't of an even darkness; it was mottled darkness. Every few yards or so an oil lamp or a kerosene torch or a Chinese paper lantern, back within some doorway or some stall opening, would squirt out a puddle of light to relieve the gloom. They were different colors, these smears, depending on the reflector they filtered through: orange and sulphur-green, and once even a sort of purple-red, were spewed around on the dirty walls, like grape juice. But don't get me wrong; it was mostly shadow; these were just the breaks in the darkness.

Shuffling figures in felt slippers and black alpaca trousers would stop against the wall to make way for us and turn and stare after us as we went by. Sometimes they tried to follow in our wake, but the rear man of our party would fang a curt word of dismissal at them and they'd drop off again.

Once a projecting sign or iron bracket thrusting out over

one of the doorways—I'm not sure which it was—clipped off my hat, but they let me stop, and one of them picked it up and gave it back to me.

We got to it. I knew it when I saw it coming from up ahead, darkness and all, even though I'd only been there once before. It was just a doorway—no show window—but it was a little wider than the others and it spilled out a brighter gash of lantern light than the rest. It had a vertical panel of black sandpaper running down each side of it, with gold-paint Chinese hieroglyphs on one side and the equivalent Spanish lettering on the other. Both were Chinese to me.

We turned off there and we went in. The alley went on the rest of the way without us, still smelling as bad as ever. In here it wasn't so noxious. It smelled of incense—dead incense, though—and of sandalwood and of stale boxes, and that was about all.

We stopped short like a three-car train, piling up on one another a little.

Acosta said curtly: "This is it, Escott?"

"This is it," I answered wearily.

"How did you happen to find such an out-of-the-way place, off the main streets, right after landing from your ship?"

"We didn't. A steerer brought us here. He kept tugging us and pestering us. Finally we let him bring us here more to get rid of him than anything else."

She hadn't wanted to come—I remembered that now—I'd been the one. I'd wanted to buy her a little present to celebrate our landfall, and I hadn't known my way around. "Let's stay out of these corner pockets," she'd urged plaintively. "The whole town's a corner pocket," I'd reassured her. "Come on, let's give it a spin."

"Himph," Acosta said. Which meant simply: *Himph.*

It looked pretty much the way it had the first time. A little deader, that was all. The same soapstone Buddhas ranged along the shelves, the same carved teakwood boxes, the same brass urns and ivory thingamajigs. The same pot-bellied tangerine lanterns strung along in a row from the rafters, each with a single black character inked on it. The same fat, kewpie-like Chinaman, with stringy white mustache braids dangling down nearly a foot from his upper lip, was dozing on the same stool over in the same corner as the first time we'd come in; sleeves telescoped across his paunch, a taffeta skullcap with a button on his pate, slippered feet tucked in behind the rungs of the stool. His handless sleeves would go up and down every time he breathed.

"Hey, *patrón!*" Acosta roused him gruffly.

A couple of little slits of eyes, like diverging accent marks, opened up in his satiny face. Otherwise he didn't move at first. You could just see a twinkle behind them; that was about all the life they showed.

"Sí señoles," he said in a singsong squeak, and busted his sleeves open in the middle. A long skinny hand came out, yellow as a chicken claw, and swept around three sides of the room. Meaning: Help yourselves. If you see anything you like, time enough to wake me up then.

That wasn't enough for Acosta. He was the police, after all.

"Take it off there," he barked, "and step over here!"

It took a lot of doing. I don't know how he'd gotten up on the thing in the first place, the trouble he had getting down. First the felt slippers unhooked themselves and dropped with a little flop, as though they were empty. He had the smallest feet for a fat man I'd ever seen. Then the belly came down next, threatening to tear loose from its moorings. Then his head and arms followed it, with little floundering gestures.

He was all down now and about shoulder-high to the rest of us. He came puttering over to us, shaking like jelly and bobbing his head ingratiatingly. He was a character. It occurred to me fleetingly he was too much of a stage Chinaman; it must have been partly an act. They aren't that way; they're just people, like we are, not bobbing Billikens. I let it go again. What did I care what he was like? The stuff that had to do with me was coming up now, anyway.

Acosta said: "You're Chin?"

He wobbled all over and beamed. He stuck a finger into himself. "Sí. Chin. At your slervice."

So the Tío prefix wasn't part of his Chinese name; I caught on. I found out later it was Spanish for "Uncle." That was his trade name or his nickname, whatever you want to call it: Uncle Chin.

"If it's going to be about me," I said, "make it in English. He speaks a few words of it. He did the last time I was in here."

He ducked his head, as at a compliment. "Lilly bit," he said. You're phony, I said to myself. Nobody could be that quaint. They'd even kill them in China if they were.

Acosta said, "Take a look at this man here."

He took a look through the slits under his eyebrows.

"Was he in your place earlier tonight?"

"Yes, gentleman was." The mustache strings rippled all the way down.

"Did he buy anything?"

"Yes, gentleman do."

"All right, tell us. What did he buy?"

"Gentleman buy knife."

That was all right; I'd never said I hadn't.

"Describe the knife. You know what means 'describe' in English?"

He simmered comfortably down over his boilers. "Oh, shu. Ornlamental knife. Knife with jade handle. For to cut letters. For to cut fluit. For to hang on wall, maybe."

"Describe the jade handle."

This was it now. I wasn't as bored as I thought I was, after all. My chin perked up a little, and I looked at him.

He brought it out in piecework. It struck me he was trying to get a buildup out of it for some reason or other.

"Jade handle have monkey."

"We know that, but describe the monkey."

His hands streaked up and blotted out the upper half of his face. "Monkey hiding eyes, so."

It hit me slow. Everything always seems to have, all my life. Like when she'd died. I'd been the last one to catch on. They were all through nodding to one another and giving the "I-told-you-so" office, Acosta and the other Cuban, before I finally got it.

Out went the ray of hope, and it got plenty dark. A bass roar that I hadn't known I possessed myself came up slow through me—all the way up from my feet, it felt like. "You're crazy! What's the matter with you? What're you trying to do to me, you fat hunk of—?" I strained forward at him from between the two Cubans who'd still been hanging onto me all this while. I upset a teakwood taboret with a lot of brass things on it, and they sang out like tocsins. "I bought the one holding its ears! You know it! You saw me—"

They shut me up. They were handling this.

"Whoa! Take it easy, now," Acosta said, and there was a glint of toughness under the calm of his manner. He forked his thumb crevice to the front of my neck and pushed me back with that. The other guy paid in his grip on my arm by twisting it around behind me, and they got me still like that.

Tío Chin shrugged amiably. "Come by threes," he said. "First one sold is to gentleman. Others still got. Can show you."

"Can lie through your teeth," I slurred at him. My arm took another quarter turn behind my back, like a crankshaft. I swallowed the rest of it. It was mostly about his mother, anyway.

He waddled over to a stock cabinet, slid back a pair of panels, and groped around inside of it. He was way over at the back, where the lantern light couldn't reach so good, anyway.

When he came back he had a roll of thick quilted silk tucked under his arm. I knew what it was; I'd seen it before. But I didn't see how he was going to prove his point by it. There *had* to be one missing, and I knew which one it was I'd walked out of here with.

"Imported from Hong Kong," he said. "Come flum there to Panama to here. Only order three sets. Cost too high; never make sale; no demand. Got invoices to show, in Spanish and Chinese. Can prove only order three sets for store. Show you invoices later."

He undid the roll first; it was fastened at both ends. Then he let it drop down, open out into a square. Or, rather, a long oblong strip. Threaded through this, on the inner side, ran a succession of silk loops, in two long parallels, top and bottom. They held a row of knives, the top ones the handles, the bottom ones the tips of the blades. All the handles were carved in the same monkey design. It was repeated three times over in three different substances: in ivory, in ebony, and in jade. There were eight: three ivory ones, three ebony ones, and two jade ones. One of the jade ones had been taken out; there was a gap where it belonged.

The two that were still in place were the monkey holding its mouth and the monkey *holding its ears*—the one that I'd bought, had had wrapped, and carried out of here in my inside pocket.

"See?" He beamed jovially.

"Well?" This was Acosta to me.

I wriggled violently all the way down, like a flag caught on a flagpole and trying to lash out. "You're a liar!" I bayed at him. "You're pulling a switch on me; that's what you're doing! I don't know how you worked it, but—"

"No do nothing," he protested querulously. "Only show this."

"Yeah, but I'll do something," I raged, "if I can only get at that stomach of yours with my foot!" It swung up harmlessly in the air; they had me back too far.

"Quieto," Acosta growled, and gave me the back of his hand across the teeth.

I didn't even notice it; I had no soreness to waste on anyone but that blubber-faced Chinaman. "You heard me ask her! You even carried that roll thing over to her, where she was standing, and held it up for her to decide! You heard which one she said to take! You saw which one I took out and handed to you to wrap! You must have done a palm switch when you carried it over to the counter—"

"I leave others there by you, in case. I only take one over to lap it up. I only loll up case after you go out of store. You touch, maybe; I no touch."

That was true; he had. That stalled me for a minute. That must have looked bad to them, checking myself like that in mid-argument. I couldn't help it. Everything looked bad to them already, so they might as well add that to it while they were about it.

Acosta sliced his hand at me disgustedly. "What is the use of stringing this out any longer? No one else bought one of these knives but you. And the one that you *say* you bought has been back here in the store all the time. Come on. We have been lenient with you, given you every chance to clear yourself, because you are a stranger here. You should have been locked up an hour ago!"

"Don't do me any favors," I mumbled sullenly.

He lingered to ask Chin an additional question or two. For the record, I suppose.

"Tell me, how did they act, these two people, when they came in here?"

"Like people do in store. No diffelent. Señola go around, touch things all over place. Gentleman stand still, not move so much."

"He asked to be shown a knife, or it was you who first offered them?"

"He ask for kimono for lady. I show; they look; they buy; I lap. Then lady, she go over in corner, touch a lot of little things some more."

"Then?" I could see Acosta getting more interested. I started to store up steam pressure for another outburst at the lies I figured were coming.

"Then gentleman, he say: 'You got something I could use in the way of a knife?' He talk low."

I'd talked low because he'd been standing right in front of me; you don't call out loud to someone when they're face to face with you.

"And?"

"I bring set; I show. He take one out; he feel to see if sharp."

Acosta was all ears.

"He go over to lady with it. He do like this."

He pretended he had a knife in his hand. He pretended Acosta was she. He drew his hand back and swiped it around toward Acosta's heart, from the side, bearing upward a little from his own hip as he lunged. "He stop just in time, before it touch her. He say: 'This is what you get.' "

"And the lady?"

"She close eyes. She say something in English. No can get; no can understand English so good."

"As if she were frightened?"

"Was frightened, maybe—don't know."

What she'd said was, "From you it'd be a pleasure." He'd taken all the playfulness out of it. He'd repeated the bare act itself, but he'd stripped it of all meaning. He'd left out the look in our eyes. How could anyone repeat that, anyway? He'd left out the playback of—I suppose you'd have to call it passion; I don't know what else to call it—from me to her and from her to me again. He'd left out the tease in my voice and the come-on in hers.

He'd sewed me up beautiful.

The explosion never came. How could it? He hadn't told them a thing that was partly untrue. He hadn't told them a thing that was wholly untruthful. I couldn't get him on it. He had me.

I kept looking at him and wondering. Did you do that on purpose? What's behind it? What do you get out of it by twisting things around that way? Or is it just my blind bad luck? Did it just happen to come out distorted that way, through the filter of your sleepy observation?

He looked so sleepy; he looked so harmless. He looked benign. That was the only word for him—benign.

They started me out. When he saw that they were through with him for the present he bobbed his head about sixteen times in parting salutation and waddled back in the direction of the stool over in the corner.

The last look I had at him from the doorway, he was perched back on top of it again, the way he'd been when we'd first come in. His felt slippers were hooked on behind the rungs; his sleeves were relocked over his belly, and those little slantwise nicks in his face had already dropped closed again. He'd drowsed off before we were even over the threshold.

Acosta broke up my baleful scrutiny of him with a swing around the other way, by the back of my collar.

"Come on, Escott," he said grimly. "Straight ahead."

"Listen," I said through my clenched teeth. "You've got me under arrest; you're taking me down to get me booked, and you're going to get me jailed. That ought to satisfy you. All I ask is one thing. At least give me the right initial; it begins with an *S*, not an *E*."

"Don't worry, you'll get the right initial," he promised. "You'll get everything that's coming to you."

CHAPTER III

WE WERE THREADING OUR way down the alley now, back to the car, and I was thinking it over. It was a funny time and place, maybe, to be thinking things over, but it was a lot better place for it, at that, than the jail cell waiting for me at the other end of this trip. I was still on my own feet and I was still out in the open. From what I'd seen of the other buildings around town that weren't jails, I could imagine what the one that was a jail was going to turn out to be like. Something from the old Spanish days, most likely, with three-foot-thick walls, and once you got in you stayed in.

I thought it over and I came to a decision. I wasn't going to any jail for something I hadn't done. I'd go to the morgue for it, instead, if that was the way it had to be. Or I'd go on the lam for it. And those were about the only two alternatives that were offered. But I wouldn't go, not even passively acquiescent, like I was walking now, into any jail.

She was gone, anyway, so what did I care? Make it tough for them. Let them work for their pinch. I had to take it out on someone, so it might as well be them.

According to their lights, I supposed, they considered they'd been fair to me. They'd leaned over backward to be fair to me. Maybe, as Acosta had said, because I was a foreigner. They hadn't even booked me yet; they'd held off until after they'd brought me around to see the Chinaman first. They'd given me every chance to clear myself, and if it hadn't worked out, that wasn't their fault; that was—well, just the breaks, I guess. They'd given me every chance but the main one—my own freedom of action. I couldn't ask them for that, so—I was going to take it without asking.

Let them drop me on the street if they wanted to; I was going to stay *out* just as long as I still stayed *up*. The only way I'd go in, if I went in at all, would be the long way, flat. And that's a handy frame of mind to be in when you contemplate making a break. It simplifies your actions.

It had to be now or never, before they got me back into that car. There were a couple more of them waiting in it, which would double the odds against me, and they'd probably handcuff me this time for the final lap down to police headquarters. Why they hadn't until now I couldn't quite make out; probably until this last finishing touch from Chin I hadn't been in a state of total arrest. Now I was. The distinction, if any, was too fine for the naked eye. But handcuffs or not, this was the place for it.

We were threading our way back the way we'd come in, Indian file, on a sort of chain arrangement. Me in the middle, Acosta behind me, the other fellow in the lead. They were both armed; I knew that for a fact. I didn't much care. My sense of values had altered now that I'd lost her. A bullet either stopped you or it didn't; either way, what difference did it make?

The car was sealing up the lower end of the lane. So forward was out. That left me a choice of two directions to bolt in: rearward or sideward into one of these moldering buildings. I had my doubts about rearward, though it should have been the natural choice to make. For all I knew, there mightn't be any upper outlet to the alley; it might be a corner pocket. I'd only get sewed up fast and pretty. It was too easy for them to shoot me, too, in the narrow chute my flight would be channeled along. The confining walls themselves would almost guide the bullets to their mark, like a sort of mortar gun bore.

That left only the sinister-looking doorways and gaps flanking our line of march. And there weren't very many left to pick from any more; the delay on my part had used most of them up; we were already getting near the alley mouth again. There were two left, one on each side of the way, both unlighted, both alike as far as looks went.

It was a toss-up. I've often wondered what would have happened if I'd picked the one on the left instead of on the right. Two doorways on a darkened alley; one spelled life and one spelled death.

I picked the one on the right.

The break was swift and silent and already over with a minute after it had begun. To succeed at all, it had to be that way. Acosta had that same double grip on me, by cuff and coat collar, as before. The man in front had me more loosely, backhand, by my opposite wrist.

I suddenly stopped short in my tracks, bent all the way over at an acute crouch. Acosta floundered across my bent back, off balance for a moment at the way he'd been telescoped into me.

I clawed around backward at him, up and over my own hunched shoulders. I got a body grip on him, pulled him the rest of the way over me, heaving with my back as well as my arms. He did a somersault to the front of me. His body came down all over the man just ahead of me, crumpled him to his hands and knees. The two of them were in a helpless, floundering mess for a minute. By that time I was already over in the doorway.

The first shot went up the empty alley, and I was already deeper in and safely off at right angles to the line of fire. My foot pickaxed into the wood of an unseen stair, and I floundered flat upon it first, then started to beat my way up it, three-legged; that is, with the aid of one hand patting its way up it in accompaniment.

They'd seen where I'd gone. They came right in after me, fast. The yellow spoke of a pocket light shot up the stairs, acting the part of a tracer bullet to the real ones that were to follow.

The second shot came an instant later, but an instant too late. I'd already made the turn-around and was out of line, just like the first time. I heard the wall substance suck the bullet in with a little popping sound, like bubble gum in someone's mouth.

I flung around the turn too wide and nearly knocked myself out against the wall on the other side, where the stairs went up again. I didn't stop; kept going, stunned, carrying a blue flash inside my head for the next flight. Then it dimmed and went out again. I made another turn, this time without collision, and started up a third flight.

The attenuated pencil of light kept whipping around after me, too late each time. It could go only in a straight line, and I could go around in a curve at the head of each flight. They were trying to catch me in it and then shoot along it at me. So it would have killed me in itself, if it had ever touched me, as surely as if it had been some sort of a shriveling death ray. But I managed to stay out of it. Each time it struck wall space, unobstructed, where there had been me a wink before.

And it even helped a little. Gave me its indirect reflection to go by, took the edge off the gloom, at least showed where there were walls and where there weren't any, revealed the coffin-shaped outlines of doors.

The third turn was the last; there weren't any more after that to break the deadly aim of the light. There was a square vent in the ceiling at the back of the passage giving on to the roof; I could see stars through it. And there was a ladder of rusty, twisted chains, wood for the crosspieces, spilling down from it. The light showed me that as it started to glow up behind me like a lethal sunrise.

I knew I'd never have time for it. If it had been rigid, maybe. But the chains would whip around with my weight and tangle me. Their arms wouldn't catch me, maybe, but that light beam and the bullets needling it would. They'd get me in the legs or better. They were nearly up now, the light welling up behind me to imminent calamity, like something about to burst.

I shied my hat over at the drop ladder. It landed at the foot of it, as though I had lost it while climbing. Then I grabbed at the knob of the nearest dark oblong and tried to push through. It wouldn't give; locked or blocked. The light was nearing full strength now, starting to tip over the rise, slide into the straightaway where it could pick me up. There was only one more dark oblong, past the first one. I tried that, felt it break away inward. I went through.

Just as I got it closed again the baleful light licked by it on the outside. I could tell by the way the seam glowed livid in the very act of closing, then dimmed again as the beam went on past.

I held my body pressed tight against it. I heard their footfalls thud quickly by, following up the beam that had gone on before. Then a smothered remark as the light picked up my fallen hat. "*¡Salío por aquí!*" or something like that. He went up this way. I suppose. Then the chain arrangement creaked as weight was put to it.

You could almost follow their ascents, one after the other, by the little thumps its loose end gave against the floor, like the tail of a busily wagging dog.

Then that stopped, and they must have been up above on the roof now.

If I'd had any faint hopes of being able to slink out again and retrace my way to the street behind their backs, they were scotched a minute later. A voice called up from the bottom of the well, all the way down at street level, asking something. One of them came back to the edge of the roof gap and called down something in answer. No doubt to stay down there and watch the entrance. That meant the other two from the car had come up at sound of the shots; I was between the two parties of them, trapped there where I was.

Palms still soldering the door seam, one high over my head, the other down lower, I turned and looked across my shoulder. To try to see what this was, where it was, that I'd gotten. There was nothing to be seen. Just utter smooth blackness all around me. Not even that relieving ray was in here with me, as it had been outside. Not a detail, not an outline visible. It was like being in a tunnel. It was like being in a grave. I turned back again, face toward the door.

But I must have brought the memory of something in that blackness around with me, to be fanned in retrospect until it glowed into meaning. For suddenly, startled and unsure, I had quickly whipped my face around once more in that well-known double take that means you're trying to catch up with something that didn't sink in the first time. That's usually done in the light, but I did it now in the bottomless dark.

I couldn't find it for a minute, and then I did. There *was* a detail visible. Just one, in all that nothingness. A red mote. A dot, hanging suspended in the air. Like a spark on the loose, but that's forgotten to finish falling the rest of the way.

I watched it for a bristly, shivery second or two. It didn't move. I didn't move either. I didn't breathe much; maybe just a little, just enough to keep the works going.

Then suddenly I got it, by dint of long hard staring at it. Or, rather, by thinking it out, more than just staring. I knew what it was: it was a cigarette end being kept alight between somebody's living lips. It had a slow, imperceptible rhythm to it when you looked long enough. It got smaller, dimmer, faded; then it came on again, clearer, brighter, larger. Breath was backing it, probably involuntary breath, like my own breathing was at the moment. Breath that couldn't be stilled entirely but that was suppressed almost to the point of cessation. There was somebody alive over there, across the dark from me, so still, so watchful of me.

It gave itself away, the red pin point. It went up suddenly, about two feet in a straight vertical line. Then it stopped again, froze there. I translated it. The smoker had risen. He was erect; he was full height now, where he had been seated or crouched or inclined before.

It was deftly done. There wasn't sound to go with it. He was trying to remain intangible, non-present to me. He didn't know he'd already given himself away. The red ember must have been an oversight; perhaps long incessant habit made him forget he was holding smoldering tobacco out before his face.

I stared, hypnotized. I couldn't take my eyes off it. It was like a red bead of danger, a snake's eye fixed on me. My spine felt stiff, and a funny sort of air-cooling system seemed to play back and forth across my scalp, under the hair.

It hung there at its new altitude for a questioning, stalking moment or two. I stood at bay, shoulder blades hinging the door seam. It dimmed a little with accumulated ash; then another unconscious suck of air brightened it up again.

It started to move again, in an undulating way that told it was moving forward, toward me. It went up very slowly this time, on perspective as it drew near, and not straight up as it had the time before. It got a little bigger, to about the size of a pea. It came on like a distant red lantern on a buoy riding a pitch-black swell.

It was spooky. It was something to get the creeps about. I got them. But I stood my ground. There wasn't anything else I could do. One of my knees started to fluctuate treacherously. I locked it, and that held it.

It was close to me now. It was up to me. It was so near to my own face that I almost seemed to feel the heat from it, radiating against my cheek in a hot spot about the size of a dime. That was pure imagination, I suppose, but that was the effect I got.

It was the silence that was so maddening—its and mine. One prolonged the other, as though neither of us—myself or this unknown quantity—wanted to be the first to make the preliminary sound that might lead, a moment after, to a death struggle. I waited for it to reveal itself; it seemed to wait for me.

I could feel my upper lip involuntarily draw back above the canine tooth on one side of my mouth; I didn't actually growl in warning, but the atavistic impulse was there. After all, the dark, the unknown; what other way was there to express cornered defiance?

My chest was taking short little dips and rises, storing in all the air it could against the coming struggle. My arms flexed, ready to grapple and slam out.

Something cool and metallically pointed found the side of my neck, right where one of the swollen, tight cords were; pushed it in a little way, and then held steady. It was sharp—sharp as the point of a pen or the tine of a fork or somebody's pointed fingernail, for instance; only just blunt enough to avoid puncturing the skin with the amount of pressure that was being applied to it. Very little more, and it would open it and slide in. Only it wasn't the point of a pen or the tine of a fork or the tip of someone's fingernail. It was the business end of a knife blade. And all it needed was one extra ounce of energy and it would go through and nail the door.

The blood couldn't travel up or down that particular cord; the pressure of the point had choked off its right of way. It dammed up below it as if a surgical clip had been applied. There wasn't a vibration or a quiver to the blade;

you wouldn't have thought it was held by hand at all, it was so steady. It was nothing to monkey around with, or grab, or fling off. It was just waiting for that, to ride home on an even keel. It was no threat; it was the accomplished act itself, but in two parts. Part two would follow immediately.

The cigarette coal vibrated a little with unseen movement. Movement that didn't carry to the knife blade, that was apart from that and left it unaffected. I had to guess at what it was.

There was a swirl of air across my steaming face, as if an arm had been swept up overhead. A second arm, not the one coiled behind the knife. Something snapped twig-like up there above eye level, and a match head creased by a thumbnail fizzed and flared out like a rocket, blinding me with its suddenness.

Then it calmed to a steadier flame and came down closer, between our two faces but a little offside, so that it didn't get in the way. The face in front of me slowly caught on in the back-shine, came through stronger, like something being developed on a photographic plate.

CHAPTER IV

IT WAS A WOMAN.

Her face glowed out at me like something transparent lighted from the inside. The typical Cuban type: high Carib cheekbones, sleek black hair parted arrow-straight up the center of her crown and twined circularly about each ear, full pouting lips, red as wet paint without there being any paint on them, biscuit-colored skin, jet-black eyes, probably large but pulled cornerwise into slits now and smoldering and dangerous behind those shuttered slits.

She had on a shawl; not your romantic Spanish-dancer thing, with roses all over it, but black and threadbare and shabby; cheap cotton, with rips in a couple of places where it had caught on nails or something. Down under one arm, up and over the other, and clinging to her person by some unaided trick of its own spiral drapery. Under it a short length of red calico petticoat peered. Under that, pink cotton stockings that didn't look any too clean. Under them, cheap native moccasins or sandals—I don't know what they were—felt or maybe straw-soled. They had no heels or arches or anything else. I didn't look down there right now; I only got that presently. I was still too busy up above, at knife level.

The match light flashed from the blade and struck into my eyes. The tendon in my neck was wearing thin. How she had managed to be so accurate in the dark, I don't know. Long practice, perhaps, in needling just the right place, sight unseen.

Oh, one other thing: the cigarette that had telegraphed her so far ahead wasn't a cigarette after all; it was a small plump native cigar, down to quarter length now, its fumes apparently inhaled along with the oxygen her system took in without once removing it from her mouth from first to last and yet without inconveniencing her, it was such second nature. A feat I defy any male cigar smoker to match.

The ash-ringed coal of it vibrated a little, and a truculent sound came from behind it. "*¿Bueno?*" I didn't know what it meant, but I could catch on by the inflection. Well? Or: What's up? Something like that. A sort of tough challenge. But the voice, harsh as it was, was a young girl's.

She said something else; I think it was: "Don't move." She whipped the hand holding the match, as though it were broken at the wrist, and there was darkness again. The knife point didn't move, I didn't move either. She must have gotten the new one from her bosom, where the shawl was at its tightest. She snapped it into combustion with her thumbnail again, one-handed, and the light came on again.

She was still waiting for the answer, I could see. The knife said she was going to get it too. She was grim; she was unfriendly.

"Take it easy, take it easy," I said. "They're after me out there. I can't talk your language. Put that thing down, will you?" But I knew enough not to gesture or even point at it; I kept it strictly word of mouth.

"Oh, an *Americano,* eh?" she said. Her underlip jutted forward in a sort of caustic purse, then flattened out again. The knife point didn't retreat a hairbreadth. It hung steady. She had perfect muscular control. And not a shadow of compunction.

I rolled my cyes to try to show her. They were the only things I could safely move, the way she had me nailed. "Cops—understand what I mean? Out there on the stairs. I don't know how to say it. *Policía.* They're after me."

She switched unexpectedly to English. And good English too. I don't mean good in the sense of high-class. Not the kind you get out of books. But the fluent kind you pick up in the gutter. "Cops, eh?" Her face changed when she said that word. A look of hatred overspread it. For me she'd had just impersonal menace; this was personalized hate.

Her eyes crackled like fuses; they stretched lengthwise, as though somebody were pinning her skin up behind her ears. "Why didn't you say so before? I hate cops," she spat.

The knife point backed out a little way. It let the indentation in my neck it had caused slowly fill up after it. It hung level there for a moment more.

"Anyone that's no friend of theirs is a friend of mine."

It dropped down all the way, was suddenly gone from between us. I don't know where it went; I wasn't quick enough. Stocking top, maybe, or some waistband under the shawl. She was fast with that thing, coming and going. For my part, all I was glad about was it was gone; I wasn't interested in finding out where.

I took my first unrationed breath in what seemed like half an hour, though it may have been only four or five minutes.

"I didn't know you talked English," I said.

"I ought to. I been in enough of your jails to take out naturalization papers," was the sullen answer.

The match was shortening up on her. She gave us the usual intermission of darkness, touched off a new one with her nail. This time she fed the flame to a stalagmite of misshapen candle stuck into the neck of a dark green beer bottle. It lifted a curtain of bleary light a few feet, leaving the top of the place, over our heads, still in darkness.

She fanned me aside with her hand, took over my place at the door seam, bent her head to listen.

"Get over there. Anyone they're after I'll do what I can for."

They were plenty active; you could hear them thumping back and forth right over us, through the lead sheeting of the roof. It gave a funny, hollow, drumlike sound, like mild thunder rolling this way and that just over the ceiling.

She hissed a soft name or two at them in Spanish. I could figure what it was: genealogical stuff.

She raised her foot lengthwise up against the bottom of the door, then scraped it down to floor level. That shot home a bolt that I'd missed seeing until now. It went into a socket in the sill. Then she turned and went across the room, over to where there was a big square of oilcloth tacked up against the wall. It evidently blotted out an unsuspected window.

It was the first time I'd seen her walk in the light. The time before, she'd walked toward me in the darkness. Until you'd seen her walk you missed the full meaning of the word "toughness." I don't know how she did it or what it was she did, but her walk was something. It wasn't hippy or sexy; as a matter of fact, she was pretty sparse; she hadn't many curves. It was more that it was antagonistic, defiant, challenging. She seemed to lock each leg as she planted it out before her, without breaking it at the knee, and then she'd sort of hitch herself over onto it and bring up the next one and do it again. It reminded me, for some reason, of a car continually shifting gears. She walked like she had a chip on her hipbone. I tried to imagine some guy taking her for a stroll down the street on his arm like that, and it wouldn't work. It was the kind of a walk that was meant to go strictly by itself, late at night, and if you were wise you'd steer clear of it when you saw it coming your way.

I thought to myself, watching her go by me, It's a good thing you're on *my* side, lady.

She spread two fingers at the side of this sort of oilcloth blackboard, stiffened her neck. "There's twenty of them down there! They're thick as bedbugs. You'll never be able to get through."

She pulled her fingers out; turned away, shaking her head. "They sure must want you bad, *chico*." She got rid of the tag end of the famous cigar that had had me so petrified before by spitting it out dead-center on the floor and killing it with her foot. Then she took out another one from the same place where she'd had the matches, down past her chest under the shawl, and got it ready by rolling it briskly between her palms. She stalked back to the candle blob and lighted up. Her mouth had been empty for ten seconds, maybe, all told, between the two.

"Do you know the town at all?" she asked me through the fog.

"Never saw it in my life before six this evening."

"You picked a good place for a jam. Where were you going to go, then, if you did get out of here?"

"You've got me," I admitted. "I was just going to go—that was all—and keep going."

She blew out another streak of skywriting. "I tried that in Jacksonville, and it won't work. You've got to have a hole to pull in after you. Either that or you've got to lam out of the place altogether. Just to keep moving is no dice; you're only heading for the police station the long way round."

"There's nothing but water around this place."

She agreed with her eyebrows. She seemed to be thinking it over.

"What're they after you for?" she asked suddenly, hugging herself tight around the shawl with both arms.

"They say I killed my girl," I told her.

"They say wrong?"

"They say dead wrong."

"That's what *you* say they say. Another man took her away from you?"

"I took her away from another man."

"Then any fool but a policeman knows, you didn't kill her. You never kill what doesn't belong to you, only what does."

"Tell them that," I muttered, ramming my hands down into my pockets.

She blew a smoke ring reflectively. "It's a heavy count, but this is still as good a place for you as any."

"I can't let you get mucked up in it," I growled. "I'll blow out again like I blew in. You don't owe me anything; why should you get loused up for me?"

She sliced off a layer of air with her hand in my direction. "Don't kid yourself. Anything I do, I'm not doing it because it's *for* you; I'm doing it because it's *against* them." She went into some Spanish again, her eyes shedding sparks in time with it.

There'd been a lull; now there was a sudden rampage again. They must have finished casing the roofs, or as many of them as they could reach. The sound of their heavy footsteps recrossing the lead or whatever it was came through to us, it was like somebody thumping on a washtub. Then the chain ladder started to sluice around.

"Here comes payday," I said.

She threw down her cigar, went into high gear. She could move fast when she wanted to. She took a jerk at my sleeve as she brushed by me. "Come here. Over here. Lie down on this cot over here. I've got an out for you. Get rid of your stuff from the waist up; take off everything."

I didn't get it, but I took her word for it. That was all there was time for. They were holding a confab, giving out instructions or something, out there at the foot of the ladder.

She dived into the gloom, over in one of the far corners of the big barnlike room. I heard a wooden drawer rasp out. "Where's that smear-stick I used to use when I was still going around with Manolito?" I heard her say.

I used the buttons on my shirt front like a zipper; just wrenched from top to bottom, and they all flew off.

They were on the last lap out there now. They were pounding on a door; it must have been the next one up from this one. Or the next one down below—I don't know which.

She came hustling back to me.

"Undershirt too," she told me.

I skinned that off me too.

"Now lie down flat there, face to the wall. . . . That's it. Keep your face pressed as close to the wall as you can. Whatever happens, don't turn around this way. Keep your arm up over your head, like that, so they can't see you from the side either. Wait a minute; first let's get this coat and stuff underneath the covers you're lying on. They may recognize that suit you were wearing."

I felt her stuffing it underneath me. Then she sat down on the edge of the cot, alongside my bared back. Without any warning something cold and slippery started to typewrite all over my back and shoulders, and down the hollow of my spine, and along the outside of one arm. I jumped at the unexpected feel of it. She pushed me flat again with a vicious swipe. "Lie still!" she hissed. "There isn't very much time."

She kept going dab-dab-dab all over me, a mile a minute. I stole a look around over my shoulder at an acute downward angle, and she seemed to be printing out coin dots all over my skin with a lipstick. I didn't get it; Quick-Brain didn't get it. When she'd hit my backbone with it I'd jump a little; I couldn't help it. It was like a spinal anesthetic.

They were in the adjoining room now. We could hear

them scuffing against the partition wall here and there as they walloped their way around in it. They were giving it a good, thorough going-over, by the sounds of it.

She flung the covers back over me, nearly to the top of my head. "Hold it, now. Don't rub against the covers. Keep your face to the wall."

She shifted the candle farther over to the other side of the room, bringing down the curtain of darkness that overhung us still lower, so that the line where the light ended and shadow began fell across me and cut me off at the neck. Then I heard her pick up some kind of a bottle standing against the wall somewhere off in the recesses of the room. An overpowering reek of some strong disinfectant welled up unexpectedly as she moved back and forth around the cot with it. I looked backward out of the corner of my eye, and she was sloshing out a few drops left over in the bottle this way and that on the floor.

They were at the door now. It almost seemed to bulge and swell inward to bursting point with the lambasting they gave it. Somebody bellowed something through in Spanish.

She made a quick pass at me, meaning: This is it now. Here we go, sink or swim. I was still glimpsing her out of the far corner of my eye. She took the shawl and elevated it, changed the hang of it, so that it draped the top of her head and her shoulders. Then she flung the end of it around back on itself, so that it covered her mouth. She looked back towards me, and I got the effect. The transformation was magical. The underworld girl had become a shrouded figure of sorrow, almost nunlike in its austerity. She even changed her walk; sort of crept submissively. She grabbed up a string of beads from somewhere as she went by—and whatever they were, they weren't religious beads—and folded them into the shawl, and after that you could hear them clicking faintly, sight unseen, while her lips moved in accompaniment, mumbling a prayer that never quite came to boiling point but kept simmering away down in her throat. Her coifed head was piously inclined.

For such short notice it was a very good act.

I rolled my face back full-compass to the wall and got the rest of it from then on by my sense of hearing alone.

She prodded up the foot latch; the door creaked wide, and there was a questioning masculine growl from two or three voices at once. The original two must have added to their number.

She went *"Shhhh!"* in a long-drawn breath of pleading remonstrance. I could even visualize her placing a cautioning finger against the shawl over the place where her submerged mouth was, but maybe she didn't.

That wasn't enough to hold them. I would have been surprised if it had been.

There was an inward surging of footsteps as they elbowed her aside and fanned out into the room. Then a halt again as they sighted me, floating half submerged in the gloom, just over the watermark of candleshine. Then a sharply barked question, obvious enough to translate itself without aid: *"¿Quien es eso?"* Who's that?

She wined a long-drawn-out answer in a weepy undertone, with sniffles for punctuation marks. All I could get out of it was the couplet *"mi hombre,"* repeated a couple of times over. My man. I was her man.

There was a pause when she got through, ominous rather than reassuring. I could feel their sharp, shrewd policemen's eyes boring into me from about six different angles at once, fluoroscoping me through the covers and all. It wasn't a very comfortable feeling. I forced myself to lie there huddled and inert, the way she'd posed me. Gee, it's hard not to move a muscle when you're dying to. It was tougher than if I'd been standing upside down on my head. The damp plaster of the wall smelled rotten that close to the button of my nose. It tickled the inside of it, too, and I was afraid the old sneezing itch that you invariably get when you're trying not to attract attention would hit me any minute, but fortunately it didn't develop.

I opened one eyelid guardedly, under the shelter of my upcurved arm, and watched the wall, like you do the rear-sight mirror in a car. The dividing line between candlelight and gloom suddenly shot way up high. I could get what that meant. One of them had picked up the candle, was holding it aloft so they could all get a better look at me.

She was remonstrating in a plaintive, melancholy voice, but that didn't do any good, it stayed up where it was.

I knew what was coming in another minute after that, and it did. A looming form started to swell upward on the wall, creeping up from below, as one of them came slowly over toward me to take a look at contact point. The nearer he got, the darker and bigger his silhouette got. The tread stopped right up against my backbone, or practically so, and he was standing there, looking down at me. I was afraid to close even the half eye that I had open now, although it was on the inside of my face, away from him.

The silhouette suddenly crumpled, foreshortened, and I knew what that meant. He was bending his head down now, to examine me from even closer quarters. I could feel his breath on a strip of my neck that wasn't covered.

If she'd only passed me that knife of hers before she let them in, I kept thinking, I might have been able to jump him, turn him around and use him as a shield against the others, force my way out right through the middle of them. No, I knew better than that. How far would I get? Down to the foot of the stairs, maybe, at best. Then I'd simply walk into the arms of those who were waiting down there around the entrance.

In a half minute now it would be all over. I almost felt like turning around of my own accord and giving up, but I didn't.

I saw the grasping, open-clawed shadow his hand made on the wall as it hung poised over me for a moment, about to come down and pull the covers back, fling me around so he could see my face.

It dipped, and I felt the covers go off me. The air played over my unprotected back, crinkling the skin.

There was a startled gasp, not just from one but from four or five different throats at once. The wall brightened; the shadow had suddenly snapped back to a distance, like stretched elastic. He must have given a backward broad jump, to move that fast.

Somebody choked out a question in a curdled voice.

I heard the girl utter a single musical-sounding word in answer. She rolled it on her tongue as though she enjoyed it. Gee, it was a pretty word. Their language is full of them, but this was so liquid, so melodious, it had even the others beat. "*Viruela,*" she said.

There was an equine scream, a whinny of dismay. Somebody else let out a hoarse yell to go with that. There was a floor-throbbing stampede of heavy feet that quivered the cot I was on, all converging toward one point, all trying to get out of the room at one time. You could hear loose arms and legs strike against the doorframe before they were pulled through after their floundering owners. The backdraft bent the candle flame over flat, teetered the whole structure of light and shadow in the room.

Then the door slammed shut like a bomb; their sound track faded to a whisper, and the two of us were alone in there again.

I could tell we were, but I didn't move for a minute, just to make sure.

They kept going, outside in the hall. The panic was on them bad. The whole rickety building seemed to vibrate with their headlong tumbling down the stairs out there.

Then a little of the clamor came up from the outside, from the front way, when they first hit the open air, and that meant they were out altogether; they were back in the alley where they'd started from.

She hadn't given me any signal yet, but I turned slowly and looked. The candle flame had only just managed to straighten up again after the suction of their exit, was still jiggling crazily. She was head-bent by the door, listening. I saw her thumb her nose at it in a sort of blanket farewell to them. She slurred something under her breath, but it was no prayer this time.

I rolled over and sat up. "Good work," I said cheerfully.

She turned around and looked at me. She gave me the wink with one of her big black eyes. "Not bad, eh?" she agreed. She dropped the shawl back to where it had been before and became the street Arab again. Funny what a little touch like that can do sometimes. She chucked the beads back into the discard.

She moved aside from her listening post, revealed a small yellow placard dangling from the doorknob that had been hidden from me until now. It was still swaying lightly on its cord from the ferocious exit slam they'd given it just now. On it, it had the same pretty-sounding word, printed in big black capitals that I'd heard her mention to them before: VIRUELA.

"Say, what is that?" I asked her. "What does it mean?"

"Smallpox," she said unconcernedly, giving the card a little flick aside with her nail. "It's a Board of Health warning to keep out. You know, a sort of quarantine sign. It should have been on the outside of the door, not in here, but they were too excited to stop and think about that. I knew they wouldn't have the guts to take hold of you and turn you over and look at your face."

"It sure did the trick." I grinned. I was sitting on the edge of the cot now, pulling my shirt down around me again, rouge spots and all. "How'd you happen to have it handy like that?"

She shrugged offhandedly. "It was left over. The sanitation people forgot to take it away with them last time they were here. You see, somebody really did die of smallpox on that cot a couple of weeks ago."

I got up off it fast, with a sort of spring; finished my dressing someplace else.

She smiled a little when she saw the querulous way I was looking over at it and dusting off my seat. "Don't worry, they fumigated everything before they left. I've been sleeping on it myself ever since, and I'm all right. It worked, anyway; that's the main thing."

"Just the same," I admitted, "I'm glad I didn't find out about it until after it was over."

She went over to one of the wooden drawers, opened it, and retrieved the unfinished cigar she'd dunked in there just before she let them in. It must have died lingeringly. A whole lot of pent-up smoke came up out of the drawer with it.

She socked the dead ash off it against the edge of the drawer, jacked it into her mouth, pulled a match out of that endless frontal reservoir she seemed to carry around with her, and lit up with a grateful sigh. She was back in the underworld full-time again. Then she leaned there slantwise, with her back and both elbows against the wooden chest.

"What do you do, smoke cigars all the time?" I asked her curiously. "Don't you ever go for cigarettes?"

She curled her lip at me. "Cigarettes are for babies. I was smoking cigarettes when I was nine years old."

"Wow," I said softly.

"I didn't inhale until I was ten, though," she qualified it virtuously.

I just took that in. That was about all you *could* do with it.

"I used to work in a cigar factory in Tampa," she added. "That's where I got used to them. About every tenth one I made up I'd smoke myself."

I was knoting my tie now, sight unseen. I kept looking at her, trying to figure her out. "Why'd you go to bat for me like that just now?" I asked curiously.

She gave one shoulder a slight push. "Different reasons. Like I told you, I hate the police. I'm always on the side that they're not; I don't care whose it is." She followed a trajectory of smoke upward with her eyes. "Flowers on a grave, I guess."

"What do you mean?"

"It's hard to explain. It's my way of doing something for someone that isn't around any more, I guess. It's the only way I have. I don't know any other way. You see, I know what it is to lose someone you love, too, just like you. It happened to me only a couple of weeks ago, right here in this same room."

I thumbed the fumigated cot. "Is that the—?"

"Yeah, that was Manolito. We were deported from Miami after we both did a stretch there. We had an old record hanging over us here, and they were just laying for us. They hounded us—him especially. For weeks and months they wouldn't let us alone. He got it in jail, where they were holding him for something they found out later he hadn't done. Then when they saw how sick he was they threw him out like a dog and let him crawl back to me here to die."

You couldn't tell how deep it went except by her eyes. They flashed like the beacon of Morro Castle on an overcast night. The rest of her face stayed impassive, didn't show anything.

I didn't know what to say. I turned away and tucked in my shirt. "What's your name?" I asked her finally, with my back turned.

"My real name? I forgot it long ago. I've got a dozen of them, one for every place I go. I'd better give you the one for this district, as long as we're in it. Around here they call me Media Noche, because I always hang around late by myself—since he's gone."

"Media—I can't say it."

"Midnight is what it means. Try it that way."

"Okay, Midnight it is, then." I went over to her and put my hand on her shoulder and gave it a squeeze. "Well, Midnight, I don't know what to say to you except—thanks."

"Flowers on a grave," she murmured, low.

I gave my hatbrim a final tug. "I better blow, I guess. The coast must be clear by now."

"You better not blow, you mean. You'll get as far as the first street corner before they spot you and jump on you again. What do you want to throw away all my hard work for?"

"I can't hang around here the rest of the night."

"Is there any other place in town you've got you can go to?"

"No, I don't know any—"

"Then what's the matter with it here?" She held out one hand, like you do when you're trying to feel for rain. "It's your life, chico. Go ahead and throw it away if you want to; it's up to you. But then in that case, why didn't you just string along with them in the first place? You would have saved yourself a lot of wear and tear."

That was right; why hadn't I? I lit a cigarette from her candle flame and went over and sat down undecidedly on the edge of the smallpox cot again. Even if it hadn't been fumigated as she'd said, I was getting used to it by now.

We hung around like that in silence for a while, while the candle burned away. Me with my cigarette and she with her cigar. Two faces in the dusky pallor, thoughtful and unaware of each other. She was thinking of *him,* I guess, and I know I was thinking of *her*. A sort of wake of the underdogs.

After some time she spoke again. "How you figuring on getting out of town, even if you do get out of this place?"

"I don't know; there must be some way—"

"If you do give them the slip on the landward side, what good does it do? You're still on the island, water all around you."

I nodded dejectedly.

"And if you try to get out by water, then you've got the customs and the harbor police to buck. They keep a closer watch on the waterfront than anywhere else in this town."

I threw my cigarette away. "It looks like I stay in Havana."

"It looks like you do. And if you do stay in La Habana, I give you about thirty minutes at the outside from the time you leave the door downstairs."

"Some future," I said.

More silence. After a while I looked up again. "It looks like I stay in Havana *and* clear myself," I told her finally. "I wasn't particularly keen on running away from something I didn't do, anyway, even if it could have been done. Once you start running you never quit running. I'm going to stay here till I've got this thing licked."

"There's no law against trying," she commented.

I started fooling around with my fingers, bending them in and out and looking at them, as if they were interesting.

After a while she changed hips against the dresser top. "You want to tell me about it?" she suggested. "We got nothing else to do right now, anyway."

So I told her about it.

CHAPTER V

I'D BEEN WORKING FOR him for a week before I even saw her, knew that she was there.

It was funny how I got the job. Picked it up out of the gutter, you might say. Symbolic, I suppose, if you go in for that sort of stuff, which I don't. That's about where a job like that would be lying, come to think of it. I wasn't even trying for it. I turned it over with my foot, and there it was.

I was in Miami. My name was Scott. That was about all I'd brought down with me. I had clothes. You get arrested if you don't. I had one article of each basic garment, all on me and in use. Nothing left over. I had a coat of tan and a park bench. That was all I had to my name. The bench *was* mine, in a manner of speaking. It belonged to the city, technically, but I'd been picking the same one each night, so I had a priority on it. Once I even drove another guy off it, made him look for another.

I used to get up early, around dawn or a little after. Dawn is beautiful in Miami. All flamingo-pink and baby-blue. But you can't eat it. I used to wash my face in a fountain there in the park and comb my hair with a broken half comb I had in my pocket and turn my coat back right side out, so the wrinkles wouldn't show. And by the time I got through you could hardly tell. Or so I hoped.

I came out of the park the morning that I got the job, and I was walking along, following up my own shadow along the pale pink sidewalk, giving it its head, watching to see where it would lead me. I passed this resort, this night spot—I think it was called The Acacias, or something like that. I didn't notice it much. Miami is a pleasure town, and it's lousy with them. But this was a little bigger and a little classier-looking than the average; that was all I noticed about it. It must have only just closed about an hour or so before. You could almost smell the heat still coming out of it, as you went by, from the night-long blaze that had gone on inside it; it had hardly cooled off yet.

There was a little strip of grass between the sidewalk and the curb, a sort of fancy border. I thought I saw something lying there in it, but the dew was flashing, so it made it hard to tell. I nearly passed it by at first. Then I changed my mind and went back and gave it a cuff with my toe. It turned over, and it was a wallet. I reached down and got it.

It was just a little bit out of true with the entrance of the place. As if somebody stepping into a car at that point, while it was still dark, had dropped it and never noticed it. It was black pin seal, with gold clasps on the corners. It said "Mark Cross" on the lining, which is a good place to get them. It had money in it, plenty, and for a minute that was all that interested me. Forty dollars, about.

I kept on walking.

It wasn't anonymous by any means. It was loaded with identification. The driver's license told whose it was right through the glossine, without even having to go into the various compartments. Edward Roman, and he was forty-four, and he lived at Hermosa Drive. And then in addition there were cards and scraps of paper with telephone numbers and disjointed memos on them, most of them meaningless and hieroglyphic except to the owner. No, it wasn't anonymous by any means.

But I kept on walking. My ethics couldn't argue with my stomach right then. I had breakfast without washing glasses first or loading trays, and when I got through there was a dollar and a half less in the wallet.

Then I let my ethics get the upper hand. It's surprising how much easier it is to be ethical when you're well fed.

I couldn't even find out where the place was until I'd asked three people. The first cop I asked had never heard of it and at least was honest enough to admit it. The second one had, but in a vague way that wasn't much good when it came to specific directions. A truck driver finally cinched it, after I'd been under way for some time. He said he sympathized with me if I was going to try to make it on foot; he would have given me a lift, but he was going the wrong way for that, coming in instead of heading out. I just kept going. It occurred to me there were easier ways to be honest, but I didn't have anything else to do with myself, anyway, so what was the difference?

It was way out. You felt like you were halfway up the coast to Palm Beach already before you finally got to it. It was something when you did get to it, though.

I'd seen these big places before. It's crawling with them down there. But this looked as though it had been laid out by someone who was all speed and no control. It had its own private driveway leading off the highway, which was why no one had been sure where Hermosa Drive was; that was it. The house was facing the other way, looking out to sea, with its back to the highway. It had its own private beach. It was an estate, let me tell you.

Anyway, I turned in and walked right down to it without being stopped or questioned, though there were a pair of signs, one on each side, warning you not to do that.

I went up the steps and stopped close to the door and rang. A colored man in a white linen jacket, like stewards wear at country clubs, opened up and looked out at me after a considerable wait.

I said, "Can I see Mr. Roman?"

"What do you want to see him about?"

I'd walked too far just to turn the wallet in at the door. "I want to give him something that belongs to him."

He closed the door again—sort of scared, I thought—and there was another wait. I had a feeling I was being looked over, but I couldn't make out from where, nor by whom, so I let it go again.

Then the same colored man came back again. "Come inside a minute," he said. There was something temporary about the permission, like a sort of tryout or screening. I could tell that by the brief inflection of his voice. He didn't say Mr. Roman would see me, or anything like that.

I went inside after him. He kept going toward a broad flight of stairs, but before I could get to them somebody suddenly got in front of me, and I found myself stopped. He wasn't anywhere near the forty-four that the driver's license had put Roman down for. He came up to about my eyebrows, but he packed a lot more bulk the wide way. His skin was the color of dried lemon peel, and with the same kind of coarse bumps in it. His hair looked like it had been given a shoeshine with one of those flannel polishing cloths the kids use. His eyes looked at you steady enough, but something had been left out of them. Either it had died out behind them, or else it had never been born in them in the first place. I wouldn't know what to call it; I'm not good at those things. Even dogs have it in their eyes; he didn't. Soul, I guess. His reminded me of shoe buttons. Or of coffee beans. Smooth, hard-surfaced; just objects.

He had on a black silk shirt and a mustard-color sport jacket hanging open over that. Bare blue-veined feet stuck into straw sandals. But you didn't feel like laughing.

Something about him gave me the creeps; I don't know what it was. It was like standing with your face up against a coiled rattlesnake. An inch away, so that the darn thing wouldn't even have to stretch its neck to fang you. You can't even back out, because that might bring it on even faster. That was the kind of feeling.

But not because of any hostility or threat he was showing. He wasn't showing any. His drawl was slow and indifferent, and he acted half asleep on his feet. Even his hands—they kept brushing into me lightly all the time, without his seeming to know it.

"What was that message?"

I didn't get him for a minute.

He sort of grazed me on the chest, on the left side, with the back of his hand.

He said, "What was that you said at the door?"

"I said I want to see Mr. Roman, to give him something that I've got for him."

"That could mean a lot of things, you know." But he didn't say it to me; he said it to the colored man waiting with one foot on the first step, one foot on the second.

His hand had been down at my hip. Or something had—too quick and deft for me to be sure. But then when I looked it wasn't any more.

He said, "Excuse me, you had a little dust on you."

I thought about it an hour later. An hour later I knew I'd been frisked. But right then I didn't.

The colored man who had been waiting on the stairs said, "Okay, Mister Jordan?" He acted like this was nothing new to him; he'd watched things like this many times before.

He said, "Okay, he can go up now."

I went up the stairs after the butler. I expected to hear that funny buzzing sound a rattler makes behind me any minute, but I didn't.

He knocked on a door up there and said through it, "Someone for the boss."

A voice answered through it. "He says all right."

The first one opened the door for me and said, "Go 'head in."

It was a big bedroom, and one wall had been practically left out. There was a terrace outside with an awning over it.

There was a man sprawled out in a deck chair out there. I couldn't see his face at first; there was a barber working over him. There was a white girl crouched on a hassock, holding one of his hands. She was taking little digs under his nails with a little stick with cotton wrapped around the point of it.

I just stood there in the middle of the room and waited.

He said, "Get those sideburns even."

The colored valet got down on one knee. I saw him take a little spooled tape measure out of the pocket of his jacket and touch it off against one side of the head, then against the other.

He said, "Quarter of an inch down from the top of each ear."

"And give 'em a slittle slant. No square corners. I hate these square corners on 'em."

I stood and waited.

All of a sudden the man in the chair said, "Ow!" and one of his knees kicked up a little. It wasn't the barber; he was standing back from him.

The girl said, "You moved, Mr. Roman."

He sat up straight in the chair and gave her a paste in the eye. He left his hand open, but he plugged it home hard. She went off the hassock and sprawled in a sitting position on the floor, with her legs still up over it.

"But you didn't," he snarled at her. "Not quick enough!"

She began to cry.

"Get out of here!" he yelled. "Before you get the terrace all damp!"

She picked up her things, and the valet hustled her across the room and out the door, with his arm across her back to keep her moving. He snatched up a bill from the dresser, on the wing, and I saw him give it to her. I think it was a ten-spot. "That's all right, chile," I heard him whisper consolingly; "you'll do better next time. Don't pay no heed. That's just his way."

Some way, I thought to myself.

Roman got up out of the chair and stretched and came into the room. He didn't look the forty-four the license had him down for, either. Toads don't show their age. He had on blazer-striped satin pajamas, purple and a very light green, about the color of a fish's belly when you look at it through the water. That was what they were; the record stands. He had a brocaded robe mercifully covering most of them, except the trouser legs and the chest; of a very intricate pattern—I think they call it Păisley.

He went over and looked at himself in the mirror. Looked at himself good. I kept thinking, You must have a strong stomach, mister. Then he picked up a cigar and clipped it and lighted it. Then he decided the time had come to notice me.

He said, "What can I do for you, Jack?"

I said, "I thought maybe you'd like to have this back," and held it out toward him.

He looked at it in surprise; didn't seem to want to believe it was his, even after he'd opened it and conned it. He said, "This ain't mine, is it? Where'd *you* get it?"

I told him where I'd found it.

He still had a hard time convincing himself. He said to the valet, "Get out my last night's. See if the wallet's missing from it."

The colored man looked. He said, "It's gone, boss. Not a sign of it."

Roman said, "I never even missed it until now!" He was

a little taut, I thought. He started to look all through it quickly, but not at the money.

Then he shot open a drawer and took out another billfold, an alligator one this time, and looked through that. "I guess it was in this one," he said. He looked a little relieved, I thought.

"How much was in it?" he asked indifferently.

"Forty-one dollars," I told him. "I spent a dollar and a half to get something to eat, so there's only thirty-nine fifty left in it now."

He said, "I wouldn't have known." He looked at the valet. "Can you imagine that for an honest guy?" There seemed to be some sort of novelty attached to it, as far as he was concerned. "Can you beat that?" he kept saying. "He comes all the way out here with it—"

He turned to me abruptly. "Take it; it's yours, fellow," he said to me.

I turned it down. "Thanks just the same," I said, "but it would be gone inside of two or three days, anyway—"

"I like you," he said. "I want to show it. What can you do?"

I gave him the rather skinny list. "I can garden a little, carpenter, drive a car—"

He stopped me on that one. "You've got yourself a job."

The man who'd stopped me short of the stairs had come into the room. Or, rather, I looked, and he was there just inside the door. He seemed to have that trick of suddenly appearing from nowhere.

He said, "What about Claybourne? D'you want two of them, Ed?"

"Can him," Roman said. "Give him twenty minutes to get out of there." Then when the two of us got to the door he changed his mind. "Make it fifteen," he called. "I may want to use the car in about half an hour myself, and I don't want to get held up."

That was on a Thursday.

I worked for him a whole week before I even saw her, knew that she was in the house at all.

The phone rang in my quarters, and Job's voice said, "Bring the car around, Scotty. Two and a half minutes, now." He was the colored butler who'd first opened the door for me the week before.

"Yep," I said.

I thought it was him again. I put on my jacket and cap and got in and took the car over beside the main house. I braked flush with the entrance and stepped down, opened the back up, and stood there by it at attention. He liked all the trimmings when he got into his car.

And the door opened and a girl came out.

By herself, and beautiful. It's all right to say beautiful, but it's not the word that counts; it's what it does to you.

I blinked, but I kept the rest of my face from showing anything.

She came out slow, as though she didn't much care whether she got to where she was going or didn't get there. Not slow so much as listlessly, wiltedly. She closed the door behind her and she came down the steps.

She didn't even look at me. Her eyes were down, their lids at half mast. I don't think she even noticed there'd been a change of drivers. How could she if she didn't look at me? I was probably just a blurred bottle-green offside to her retinas.

I got her by heart between the entrance steps and the car step. By heart is right.

She wore a cream flannel dress, one of those things that's practically a slip; no shape to it, just straight down from shoulders to knees. It had a sash of Roman-striped ribbon twisted around the waist. And she had a bandanna or kerchief of the same striped stuff knotted about her head, so that you couldn't see her hair at all or even tell what color it was. It was completely hidden. The two wings of the knot it was fastened in perked up one on each side of her head and reminded me for some screwy reason of a kitten's stubby ears. Her right hand was heavy with a diamond that must have tipped over a mountain when they mined it out from under it.

I was already taking prophylactic measures in my own mind, though. I must have had a hunch I needed them. I thought to myself, I can about imagine the type. His speed. Sure, on the outside, beautiful. On the inside, sawdust.

She said, "In toward town, please," in a low voice that you could hardly hear, and got in.

I closed the door after her. She sat down on the seat with that little precautionary under-leg tuck they give even the scantiest of skirts. Ever watch them?

I got in and drove her. He liked it fast. I took it moderate with her. But she didn't seem to know or care how we were going.

On the way in she said suddenly, "Stop here a minute."

I stopped, but when I looked around there wasn't anything there but the sea. But it was a particularly good place to see it from, a secluded place, with palms framing it on both sides.

We just sat there; I don't know how long. I watched her in the glass once or twice. She just kept looking out at it. Looking out at it. She was straining slightly forward. She even had her two hands on the car-window sill. There was a yearning, wistful expression on her face, like you'd see on the face of a shut-in peering out from behind a window at the world outside.

She was just looking out at that line where the water met the sky. That imaginary line that isn't there when you get to it but that promises so much to all of us.

You couldn't hear a sound from me. A change of opinion doesn't make any noise. I quit fidgeting on the driver's seat, like I'd been doing until then, and just looked down at my own lap and stayed that way.

After a while we went on, and she finished her shopping or whatever it was, and I waited for her and brought her back.

On the way back she spoke to me twice. She said suddenly, "What happened to Claybourne?" As if she'd only just then discovered that she wasn't riding behind the same man.

"He's gone, miss."

She said, "It's Mrs. Roman."

The surprise was a double-header. Her being it. And then the way she said it. The look on her when she said it. I'd taken it to be just a one-season stand of his. Or maybe even a one-night stand. But it was for her whole life. And she said it in the apologetic, almost shame-faced way in which a woman who is discovered at some messy household task would say, "I'm all covered with grime and soot; I'm not fit to be seen."

That was all; not another word. And if she'd come out to the car slow, when she left it she went in twice as slow. She almost dragged.

Then Job's voice on the phone again. "The car, Scotty. Two and a half minutes." And the drive again, and the stop again.

She said, "Stop here."

I don't think it was actually the same spot. But the principle was the same.

I watched her in the mirror, puzzled. I didn't have it right for a minute. I almost thought she was frightened, or didn't feel well, until I got it straight. She was taking such deep breaths. I could see her chest rise and fall with their slowness and depth. Like a person who couldn't breathe freely until now, until she came out here to this lonely spot; who is starved for air, hungry for it, and can't get enough of it. Like a person who was trying to drink in that invisible line out there that held her eyes so fast.

On the way back she spoke to me twice again.

She said, "By the way, what's your name?"

"Scott, miss." Then I remembered about the day before and I said, "I'm sorry; I forgot," and I answered it over again. "Scott, Mrs. Roman."

"That's all right," she said, more to herself than to me. "I think I like it better the other way, at that."

We shouldn't have stopped there at sunset. They say moonlight is risky, but sunset is dangerous too. There was no moonlight for her. The spotlights on the floor shows at his clubs were the only moonlights she knew. But we stopped there at sunset, and twilight's a sad hour; the day is dying, and your hopes are dying, and your youth is dying, and the dream you've had will never come true now.

I saw the watery fill in her eyes. Her face wasn't twisted up any. The tears were just coming down it slow, the way it was, two to a side.

I should have minded my own business. It's easy to say that. I turned around to her on the seat and asked her, "Is there anything I can do?"

The look she gave me skinned my heart alive. "Yes," she said. "Make it three years ago. Push it back so that it's three years ago. Or if you can't do that, call me 'miss.' Or if you can't do that, just look the other way."

All of a sudden I'd gotten in the back seat with her before I even knew it was coming on myself.

I said the things you say when it hits you like that. Or the things you say, they said themselves.

"I love you. I've loved you for three weeks and two days now. I've loved you ever since you first got into the car in back of me. I didn't know it until just now."

I took time off and took my lips away from hers and said, "I'm sorry, it won't happen again. I'm quitting tomorrow."

She said only five words. And five were all she needed to say. It told me the whole thing. "Don't do that to me."

We didn't say anything more about it from then on, ever again. About being in love, or loving one another. We didn't have to *say* anything about it after that. We *were* it.

Three days later, when we were out there again, I said: "Look, I haven't got anything."

"That's what I want, your nothing."

"Are you sure?"

"I'm sure. I'm only waiting for you."

"Where? Where do you want it to be?"

She looked out at that line again over my shoulder. "What's over there? Over that way?"

"Havana, I think. Not straight out, but down that way a little."

"I don't care what it's called. It looks so open, so free. So *clean*. No one can get you back again, with all that deep water in between—"

"Havana, then?"

"Havana, then."

"There's a cruise ship from New York standing in right now. It goes on to there next. I'll find out when it pulls out. I'm afraid to take a chance on a plane; you have to wait for reservations. And they have a habit of phoning you to confirm or cancel the flight. It might get to him by mistake. The ferry's risky too. It's slow, and he has that cabin cruiser down in the bay."

"Don't take too long. Hurry, hurry. There's death at our shoulders all the time. Every minute, every second. Even when we sit here like this. Don't look at me, don't breathe, don't think—until we've done it."

I thought of that coiled rattlesnake, Jordan, and the lethal buzz I still expected to hear, even when I had him in the seat behind me. She was right; there was a lot of death around. Around us all the time.

"It may be soon. I've noticed it since Wednesday already. The ship, I mean. They don't stay in longer than three or four days at each stop. In case I don't get a chance to tell you tomorrow afternoon, how will I be able to—?"

I could feel her whole form quiver against me. "Don't come near me! Be careful. I'm so frightened, Scotty."

"Can you see my window, the window of my quarters, from where your room is in the main house?"

"Yes. And I've often watched it before I knew what this was coming on. It was like a little postage stamp of light across the grounds."

"I'll blink my lights then. Watch for them. When you're up there dressing for dinner, around seven. Count the number of times they go out. That'll give you the hour it sails. If it leaves before the next afternoon's drive. If they don't go out at all, that means it doesn't leave for another twenty-four hours. Then watch for them the following night."

"Take me back now. It's way overtime. And he already said to me the other day, 'You go out more in the car than you used to.' It hasn't clicked yet, but it will sooner or later; it's bound to."

I took him in the morning. And that's when I did it. I used up the slack I had waiting around for him and went over there to the place where they sold the tickets. It was due to sail at midnight that very night, they told me. I told them I just wanted space from here to Havana. I wouldn't have got it, but they'd dropped off a few people just now in Miami. I took two cabins, one for her and one for me; don't ask me why. If we'd wanted just a cheap affair we could have stayed right here and gambled with our lives and had one. We wanted more than that, and wading through a lot of muddy water didn't seem to me to be the quickest way to get to it.

I didn't see her in the afternoon, didn't have a chance to tell her. He kept me down there with him the whole time. I don't know if it was purposely done or not. His face didn't show anything. It might have been just a coincidence. And then again I remembered what she'd told me he'd said, about her using the car more often than she'd used to, and wondered. All he said was, "Stick around." So I stuck, afraid that if I made a move while his back was turned I'd give the whole thing away; and the hours piled up and rusted away into sundown.

I brought him back with me at six—fast, like a bullet, like he liked to be carried anywhere—and we streaked by that grove, *our* place, where we had stopped so often, at such speed that it was just like a quick snapshot on our right, there and then gone again.

But a funny thing happened. At the exact moment we did so Jordan broke a sour sort of chuckle in his throat. Jordan was always with him, of course; when I speak of "him" I meant it in the plural; he never moved a foot without him.

They hadn't been saying a word just ahead; there hadn't been anything to lead up to it. It seemed to come by itself, just as we were passing that place.

"What're you snickering about?" Roman asked him.

"I was just thinking," I heard him say. "That's a good place for lovers back there."

Roman didn't answer; let it go. I could feel that funny needling feeling you get when a whiff of cold air plays over the back of your neck. I curbed an impulse to raise my eyes to the mirror. I had a hunch if I let them go up to it I'd find Jordan's already there, waiting to meet mine. Maybe I was wrong, and since I didn't try it, I have no way of telling. But if it was a coincidence again, it was a very fine-drawn one: that he should laugh at that one particular place along the whole length of the road from Miami out to Hermosa Drive. To me it was as if the rattles had given a flickering stir behind me just then, a preliminary to motion.

It was dark when we got out. I took the car in as soon as they'd left it and went up to my room. The next two hours were the toughest I'd ever lived through. I paced back and forth there in my quarters, watching the time, stopping every other lap to look out the window. Away off in the dark, looking much farther away than they did by daylight, for some reason, I could see the short string of lighted beads, stretched out across the upper surface of the main house, that were the windows of his room and of hers, forming a continuous line. I couldn't signal while his lights were still on, for if I could see over there, he could see over here.

I wondered if they were having a row or something tonight. Seven came and passed, and by seven on other nights, they were usually down at the table already. Then I thought maybe he'd gone down but had forgotten to turn out his room lights behind him. But if he had, she would have stepped in and done it for him, to clear the way for me, I figured, so it couldn't be that.

I nearly went nuts. Sure, we had five hours yet, but she didn't know that; I had to get word to her. She might think it wasn't leaving until the next day, go to bed or something soon after dinner; she'd told me she did that as often as she could. In the dark, at least, she didn't have to see him; I suppose that was it.

Then, suddenly, at about seven-twenty, during one of my turnarounds between laps, half the lighted beads were gone. When I got back to the window only her lights were left. I jerked myself over to the switch, reached for it with my thumb, held off for a minute, and then started to shuttle it up and down. Twelve times I blinked it, starting with "on" and ending up with "on" again.

Then I went back to the window again and watched.

The beads blinked just once. Then they stayed on again, as evenly as before. She'd seen. She'd got it.

I went over and ate with Job, downstairs in the back, like I did every night. I was more cut off from her there, right in the same house, than I was back in my own quarters. Back there, at least, I could see the rooms she was in from the outside.

"It's like a funeral out there," he told me with a jerk of his head toward the swing doors. "Chills the food before you even set it down."

I didn't answer. That's a hell of a word to come up tonight of all nights, I thought. I only hope it's the wrong one.

"You haven't eaten much," he told me when he got up to scrape the plates off into the pail. Then he added, working away at it, "*She* didn't either, tonight. Scarcely touched nothin'."

This time I shot him a look, a long sharp-pointed one, to see if there was any meaning hidden in the hookup he'd just made between us. There didn't seem to be any; he would have answered the look if there had been. I think. They always look to see where the thrust lands when they've made one. It must have been just a coincidence, like Jordan's laughter at the moment of passing the palm grove.

I got up and shoved my chair back and went back where I belonged. This was about a quarter to nine. We had about three hours, now. Two hours net, deducting the ride in.

I was nervous. I'd never been so nervous before. All the little lines across the flats of my hands were wet and shiny, and no matter how many times I dried them off, they'd come back slowly wet again. It wasn't fear *of* those two—Roman and Jordan—as much as it was a fear *for* her; that I mightn't be able to get her out of there in time; that she'd suddenly be held fast, immovable; that I'd lose her; I guess that was it. A sort of love anxiety.

I walked around and around; how I walked around! There should have been dust coming up under my heels, the tracks I made.

Nine-thirty, quarter of ten, ten. Two hours left, one hour net.

Then suddenly it rang and nearly took the top of my scalp off. Job's voice: "Bring the car around, Scotty. Right away."

This was it. She must have rigged up something, found some way of—I smashed my cigarette out and ran downstairs and almost backed the car out without clearing the door out of the way first.

I got over there fast, almost too fast to stop in time.

Just as I drew up the light flashed on over the house entrance and the door opened, and she came out. She was in evening dress, white and long and glossy, and she had all her diamonds on. Everywhere they'd go, there was a diamond, and he hadn't left any place out. It was like a mass of living quartz coming toward you through the electric-light rays.

My insides all went down. I thought, There's something wrong. That's not the way she'd dress to make a quick run for it with me. My God, she'll light up the whole road into town like a flare.

Her face was frozen; she didn't know me. I held the door for her, and she passed me by and got in.

"Look out. They're right behind me."

Roman came first, bulky and perfumed up with hair tonic. A white silk scarf folded flat around his neck, but without any topcoat over it. He thought they could be worn by themselves.

And then there was a stage wait and I heard him complain, "What's Giordano doing?" And when he gave him his real name, his pre-prosperity name, like that, he was out of humor about something—but not necessarily with Jordan himself. I'd already learned that sometime back.

"Checking his bullets, I guess," I heard her say with softbreathed bitterness.

Then the rattlesnake came out, erect on its tail; the height of a man, and slim, and deadly.

They sat on each side of her, and I closed the door without meeting her eyes and hopped in.

Roman said, "The Troc, Scotty."

That was one of his places.

I took them at his pace, not hers, and the stars throbbed a little with it. I kept my eyes off the mirror. It wasn't as tough that way. I just watched the road sizzling toward us, like water lathering out of a broken hydrant.

None of the three said anything. They didn't say anything for almost three quarters of the way in.

Then finally Roman remarked, "You're quiet tonight."

She said, "I feel that way."

Jordan said, "Maybe she didn't want to come in with us tonight, Ed."

But she didn't answer.

Roman said, "Didn't you?"

"You already asked me that back at the house," she said. "I came. I'm here. What more is there?"

And after that they didn't say anything more for the final quarter of the way in. Quiet drive.

We got to the Troc with its peppermint-striped awning stretched out to the edge of the sidewalk and blue lights shining under it. The doorman, a big Bahama buck named Walter, who looked even blacker in the blue light than he was, knew who Roman was and practically got down on two knees and kow-towed.

She didn't have a chance to say anything to me. She had to alight before them, and they brought up the rear, walling her in. I watched her go in. Her white dress looked blue now, and the beautifully sculptured skin of her back looked like marble with a faint bluish tinge to it.

Everything was blue around that entrance. Even my heart.

I drove around the corner and parked there, just out of sight. I didn't know what to do. The side of the place lined the side street I was on, but there were no openings along that wall, no windows, it was just blank stucco.

I kept walking down as far as the corner and casing the entrance from there, along the frontal building line. People kept coming in all the time. No one left. The place was only hitting its stride.

Once a waiter came out and stood there a minute with Walter. I thought maybe she'd sent some message out to me. I started down toward the two of them, to make sure he wouldn't miss me, if that was it. He looked at me coming along—the waiter—and then he turned around and went in again. So he must have just wanted a breath of air.

I turned and went back. I already knew you couldn't see into the place from out front—there was too much depth of entryway—so I didn't even try.

Eleven came, and then eleven-ten. Eleven-twenty, and then eleven-thirty. I stood there by the car and I kept whacking at the glossy surface of it with my open hand. It smarted, but not half so bad as just standing there helpless, watching the time go by. Maybe that was why I did it.

Suddenly there was a shiny flash down at the corner, where there'd been only dull reflected blue light until now, and she was coming running toward me. She was just in her bare dress. I mean she'd left her head scarf and evening bag and all the rest behind her in there.

I hurried her the last few steps with my arm curved to her back. "Quick!" she panted. "Don't talk now! Just let's get away from here."

She jumped into the front seat, and I was already under the wheel.

We tore away from there.

"How much time have we?"

"Twenty minutes."

"I couldn't leave the table any sooner. I would only have had to come back again. They picked one right in a line with the entrance, damn it. They would have seen me come out of the powder room and go for the door; they were both looking that way."

"Then how did you—?"

"Someone came over and sat down with us just now. They rearranged their chairs to make room. That turned them partly the other way." She reached down into the top of her dress. "Here, take this," she said.

It was money in a small chamois pouch. She took it out and tried to hand it to me. I kept my hands on the wheel. "Whose is it?"

"Mine."

"But whose was it before that?"

She thought about it. "You're right," she said.

She put her hand on the outside and let the wind peel it away from her. It went streaming backward into the night, in tens and twenties and, for all I know, hundreds. Someone had a good time along that stretch of roadway the next day, I bet.

"Aren't we ever going to get there?"

"Soon. The worst is over now. It doesn't sail until twelve, and we still have—" I felt her pressing herself against me. "Why're you so scared?"

"That isn't it, Scotty, they *know!* The whole thing worked out wrong. It paid off ahead of time. It's delayed action with a fuse. And we've got to beat the fuse to that boat. And I don't think we can now."

I asked her what she meant. It was just a mess of words to me.

"Somebody saw you. Somebody that knows him saw you buying the tickets, or coming out of there, or whatever it was. He recognized you, or rather Ed's car. One of those ghastly coincidences, tonight of all nights. He was the one who sat down at the table with us just now. Only he thought it was Roman and me you were buying them for. Thought we were going away on a quick trip or something. I heard him mention it to Ed. Luckily it didn't register. Because I was still there at the table with them.

Ed passed it off; it didn't make sense. He thought it was just a mistake. But *now*. Starting in from the minute I left that table, from the minute they miss me—it'll suddenly make sense. It'll suddenly pay off. They'll *know*. Havana. The boat. There's only one every ten days. With the two of us gone, they'll know who the tickets were for; they'll know where to catch up with us before we have a chance to sail."

"But I have the car."

"This third man who sat down at the table with them has one of his own. They may already be on the road behinds us."

I gave it the gun. "We'll take care of that."

But now our anxiety had reversed itself. We wanted it to leave soon; soon and fast. Only give us time enough to get aboard and then pull right out.

"We'll be under way in ten minutes now."

"But you can die in only one."

"We won't," I promised her. I hoped I was right.

"There's *something* back there. *Some* pair of lights that seems to do everything we do. Awfully far back, though. The size of little pills."

"Don't keep looking back," I soothed her. "That won't keep them off our trail, if it is they."

We got there at six to midnight, with a great slashing turn and a plowing stop in front of the pier. I gave her the tickets, said: "Here, wait for me by the gangplank. I'll get this out of the way." She wanted me to come right with her, but I waved her on. We couldn't leave it standing right there; it would have been a giveaway to them, if it was they behind those distant "pills" she'd mentioned.

I took it offside, left it where it was good and dark, came chasing back on foot. Cars were coming up every minute, coagulating into a sluggish single-file line in front of the embarkation point. I couldn't tell if the "pills" were included in it or not; they had lost their separate identity. Most of the people spilling out of them were lushed up; this was a pleasure cruise, after all. The vessel's steam siren let go with a dismal, bronchial blast that drowned everything else out for a minute.

I found her waiting at the foot of the gangplank. There were plenty of other women in evening gowns milling around, and that was all to the good; it made her less conspicuous. We showed our tickets and went scampering up. A steward took us in charge, led us down below, showed us where the two staterooms were: one opposite the other across the passage. He tried to come in, adjust the porthole. I handed him a bill, said, "Never mind that. We like everything just the way it is." He turned and went off.

She said, "Lock the door." And she crowded up against it and flattened it with her hands, to make it stick fast, after it was already locked.

"I've got another one for myself," I told her.

"Oh, don't leave me. Propriety be damned. Stay in here with me tonight."

Motion started in.

I said, "It's all right. We're safe."

"I don't think we'll ever be," she said. "Do you?"

"Do you feel it? It's getting stronger every minute. We've made it. We're okay."

We sank down together on a sort of settee under the porthole, with the fresh breeze coming in over us, and we stayed that way, my arm around her, her head against mine. We stayed up all night. It was only an overnight run, anyway.

That's a pretty condensed love affair. One night. But we weren't gypped. I think we said everything there was to say in that one night. And maybe it was better there was a deadline on us. Because there was no money. And the hard grind would have chipped all the glamor off in the weeks and months to come. We had it brand-new from the factory. And what more can you ask for?

We stayed like that all night, her head pillowed on my shoulder, mine slanted back against the stateroom panel. The porthole curtain rippling inward over our heads like a pennant, the water humming softly by outside. We were happy. We were heading for that line way out yonder, where the water meets the sky, that we'd longed for from the shore.

The porthole paled, and the day broke across the Gulf Stream.

Then suddenly there was a sound at the door, and we both died a little all over again. It was about six; it was too early yet to be in Havana, and there was this soft, almost surreptitious tapping on the wood. As though it were being done with just one finger.

We were erect now but still cleaving together. I carried her with me that way over toward it.

"They're on board! They must have got on last night!"

"No, no, take it easy. They wouldn't have waited this long if they were."

We stalled to see if it would come again. It came again.

"Who's there?" I asked gruffly.

A man's voice said: "Wireless message, sir."

That's the oldest gag in the world. On land it's a telegram.

"Don't open," she whispered fiercely.

I said, "Shove it underneath if you have one."

A tongue of tawny yellow started to lick through. It really was one.

I waited until it had fallen still. Then I pulled it free, and we opened it and read it together. The instructions were to deliver immediately.

It was addressed to her. It was short and bitter. Just one word.

LUCK.
ED

CHAPTER VI

WHEN I'D FINISHED TELLING it to her the candle flame had wormed its way down inside the neck of the beer bottle, was feeding cannibalistically on its own drippings that had clogged the bottle neck. The bottle glass, rimming it now, gave it a funny blue-green light, made the whole room seem like an undersea grotto.

We'd hardly changed position. I was still on the edge of her dead love's cot, inertly clasped hands down low between my legs. She was sitting on the edge of the wooden chest now, legs dangling free; that was the only difference.

After I'd stopped I couldn't help thinking: How long it takes to live your life, how short a time to tell it.

She'd listened to it; a stranger hearing a stranger's troubles. I could hardly see her any more; she was nearly as invisible now again as she'd been earlier at our first never-to-be-forgotten confrontation. Just a light shield over there for her face, and an occasional glint coming from it for her eyes.

Silence fell, and we kicked it around between us for a while.

Then she dropped her feet to the floor with a light thud and came over and put in a new candle. A new stump, rather, but the light turned yellow again, and the fungus color faded from the walls.

"It's easy," she said.

I didn't know what she meant for a minute.

"It's easy to see what it was that happened to you in

Sloppy's tonight. Anybody with half a head can figure that out."

I kicked up my chin without raising my eyes to her.

"Figuring it out is one thing, proving it another. You mean Roman, don't you?"

"She was his; you took her away from him."

"He's in Miami. You could pick up the phone right now and call his number there, and he'd get on at the other end."

"Sure. That doesn't change anything."

"I know that as well as you. But who cares about remote control? It's the mechanics of the thing at this end that I've got to worry about." I plowed through my hair. "I still can't see how, in all that crowd around us, there was nobody who noticed the knife being driven into her. Or at least saw it in the guy's hand, whoever he was. He couldn't just hold it still and push from scratch. He'd have to draw it back, at least equal to its own blade length, and then drive it, like you do with any pointed weapon. How is it nobody saw his arm swing, saw the thing gleam?"

"Maybe," she tried to help me out, "somebody did and hasn't told about it."

"Or maybe," I said, "somebody did and doesn't know it yet."

She looked at me, puzzled. "What do you mean?"

I'd gotten to my feet, staring fixedly. Not at anything she could see, but at something I could. "Wait a minute; I think I've got something. I think I've found a possible out for myself, if it will only pay off!"

She came in closer, ready to help me.

"Let me see if I can get this straight," I said, "before I start getting steam up over it. Got something I can draw with?"

"Only that lip pencil I used before."

"Anything."

She brought it over with a couple of quick long strides.

"Can I use your wall?"

"Shoot."

I went over to it and dashed off four hurried lines that closed up a square. She came up behind me and held the candle-bottle by my shoulder so we could see better. "There are four sides to any position. These are the four sides around us where we were standing. This is us, in the middle." I scratched a hasty X. "Now let me see if I can remember how it went. On one side there was the bar. That'll be in this line here. That cut us off at elbow height. It didn't go in from there anyway; it went in on the other side of her."

"Make an arrow to show which side it went in from," she suggested.

I made an arrow hitting the X. "Now on these two sides —the arrow side and the side here, behind the two of us— they were packed all around us like sardines. Their own bodies hid the knife play from them; it went on out of sight down in between somewhere. But there's one side left, this fourth side here. *That's* the one side where there was a little clearance—only a few feet, maybe—but still a little opening. You can always see things better from a short distance off than when you're right up next to them—on top of them, you might say. That's the side I'm counting on. That's the only side that had any kind of perspective on us at all."

"And who was on that side—more of the crowd?"

"There was only one guy blocking off that entire side— the photographer that works Sloppy Joe's. Now do you begin to get what I'm driving at? The crowd was there, yes, but backed up behind him. He had this black hood, or whatever it is they use, spread out, cutting them off. He *was*, for all practical purposes, the entire fourth side. The whole opening was only a tiny thing, anyway."

"Then you think the photographer saw it?"

"Not at first hand. His own head was down under the blamed hood. But I think there's a good chance his camera caught it. And that's the one witness that doesn't lie, that can't be fixed—a camera plate."

She didn't act any too sure. "It goes like this." She gave her fingers a snap. "It would have to be awfully fast. The two of them would have to come right—like that— together."

"It doesn't have to show the actual moment of incision. First he had to get it out, then he had to strip the wrappings, then he had to poise it, then he had to shoot it in, then he had to leave it there. That's five or six different steps. It could have got any one of those, and it would still be just as much help to me. It all depends on how much of us he got into focus.

"The knife went in down about here." I showed her where, on her own figure. "If he took us just head and shoulders, he missed it; it was too low. But if he took us at half length—say from the waist up—there's a good chance something may show on his plate. Even if it's just enough to show that it wasn't my own hand holding the knife, but somebody else's, that's all I need. At least it'll be a lot better than what I'm bucking now."

I flipped the lipstick over onto the cot.

"He's still got that plate with him, in the back of his camera or somewhere!"

I buttoned up my coat and started for the door. "I'm going. I only wish this had hit me sooner. I've got to find out who he is and where I can get hold of him again!"

She parked the candle, got over to the door ahead of me, turned, and motioned me back.

"You better let me tackle it. I can do it for you, and a whole lot quicker and easier than you can. You'll only be sticking your neck out."

"You've done enough for me already. This is my own jam, not yours."

She gave me the back of her arm in rebuttal. "You can't even talk the language; how you going to ask anyone? Where you going to go looking for him—around Sloppy's? You can't even show your face around there without getting picked up. Talk sense, chico, will you? I can do it in half the time. Nobody knows me or thinks I have anything to do with you. I can come and go like I please. Sit here quiet, now. Lock the door after me and don't open it up for anyone. I'll knock like this, double, when I come back, so you'll know it's me." She showed me how.

"I feel like a heel," I said, "letting you do my dirty work for me."

"I'm not doing it for you. I'm doing it for a guy the cops were once down on, just like they're down on you now. Flowers on a grave. How many times do I have to tell you? Stay here; I'll be back as soon as I can."

The door opened narrowly; she peered, slipped through; it closed again and she was gone.

I stood there listening to her go for a few minutes; you could hardly hear her, just a soft whisper going down the stairs. Then I kicked down the latch with my foot and turned away and ambled across the ghostly, candlelit room.

I sank back on the cot and sat there, thinking. Thinking what a honeymoon this had turned out to be. *Her* on a slab at the morgue and me hiding out in an outcast's room in the Chinese quarter.

Time seemed to stand still, just hang there, stuck. I had no watch to nudge it along—I'd never had one in my whole life, now that I came to think of it—and there wasn't anything in the room to go by either. Only the slow, slow sinking of the candle flame, and I didn't have the knack for turning that into numbers. Once in a while I could hear faint, far-off churches here and there across the town jangle thinly like plucked wires, but I couldn't make head or tail of them either. They weren't even; one would start in just as another was getting ready to finish, and that would run the score up higher than there were hours in any night. I couldn't tell where one left off and the next began. What did it matter? I had no date.

Then all of a sudden I heard something, and my neck went up. Nothing moved in the whole room for a minute except the cigarette that dropped in a plumb line from my fingers to the floor, and the foot that pinned it where it had fallen.

It was someone on the stairs, and for some reason I had a good hunch it wasn't she. I think it was the rhythm of the tread told me; it was slower than hers. True, I'd never listened to her climb before, had never taken the count of her footfalls, but somehow I felt she would at no given time have come up any stairs with that lethargic, almost somnambulistic beat. The rhythm of the walk is an index to each personality; it is as distinctive as fingerprints or the timbre of the voice; no two alike. Hers might be as stealthy as this, as soft-purred, particularly if she were stalking someone, but there wouldn't be that excruciating lag between each drop. Almost as if the climber had frozen each time before going on to the next pace. It didn't match her.

There was no leather in the texture; it was the slurred sibilance of felt, such as in those moccasins she wore or the slippers that the Chinese featured around here. It should by that token have been altogether inaudible, but it wasn't; there was enough grit upon the aged stair surface and enough hardened coating of wear upon the underside of the sandal to give that little whispered betrayal each time they ground together. Particularly in such a silence as this, and to such wary, hunted ears as mine.

I was erect now at a crouch, holding the cot frame down by my palms along its edge to keep it from singing out as I left it. I let it up very easy, and it grumbled only a little.

It had left the stairs now, was coming on toward the door on a flat plane—don't ask me how I knew; you can tell things sometimes without being able to tell afterward how you told at the time.

I started to cross the room in time with it, fitting my own stifled paces into its falls out there on the other side, so that the one might possibly cover up the other, just as those church bells had confused me before.

I pinched the candle flame dead between my fingers in passing, and then I was at the door. Like I had been before, when I first came in here. But the police had been easy to figure; you knew where they were heading from a mile away; this you couldn't tell what it was.

It went: *Sh*—one—two—two and a half; *sh*—one—two—two and a half. About like that. It might have been a palsied totter, as of someone about to fall flat on his face between each step, but I wasn't counting on that. It might equally have been somebody very sneaky, but not quite sneaky enough, trying to get up within grappling distance outside a door before he was detected.

It stopped. The two and a half ran up to three, four, five, and the break didn't come. It must be right out there in front of my face, at a halt.

A part of my coat moved a little against my body, and the shock was like that of feeling a weapon's touch go against you. I managed to hold still, and then I saw that it was the knob trying to turn and carrying the goods of my coat partly around with it, where they were pressed close together.

Then a hand tested the door for give, pushing at it here and there to force it through. There was a sharp, scratching sound that made me jump as though it had opened my skin; it was the head of a match being carried across the door to ignition point. The seam suddenly stood out, as though a long yellow thread had been unraveled.

But this was no longer as furtive as the approach had been, and it reacted in kind upon me. The tension I had been under channeled itself suddenly into a desire to come to grips, to retaliate. She had told me not to open the door, but you're always your own man when you get sore enough.

I toed up the foot grip, ripped the yellow threat of the door seam wide, and braced myself to crash into whoever it was. And then I didn't. There are some figures that are too awesome even to tangle with in fight. This one was so uncanny I couldn't have brought myself even to touch it, much less hit it or grab at it.

I couldn't tell if it was a ghost, or something alive that had come up out of the grave, or something already dead that was on its way down into the grave and had stopped off here first by mistake. It was an emaciated, cadaverous-looking Chinaman. I couldn't tell if he was old or young. The match rayed down over him, but its rays didn't make any too much sense. He wasn't white and he wasn't yellow either; the color of his face was a grayish green. His eyes were sunk in deep pockets, as big as the sockets in a skull. His clothes hung loose on him, like the rags on a scarecrow. He must have been just tined ribs under them, without any skin to web their dorsal projections together.

A curious sort of odor came from him, like—well, there's a certain sort of clay; if you mix it with water it gives that same brackish, pottery-like reek.

He acted stupefied. He said something between his teeth, but I couldn't get what it was. *"Otla puelta."*

"Beat it," I cursed low. "Get out of here, you walking spook!"

He turned uncertainly, like he was going to fall over any minute, and started to feel his way along the wall with one hand, toward the next door down. The match went out before he got there, and I closed the door and fastened it again. He was bad enough in the light; I didn't want him coming back again in the dark.

I listened warily and I could hear the other door softly open and close again. Sounds of someone moving quietly around in the adjoining room filtered through the partition for a minute or two after that, and finally complete silence descended, as though the thing had died in there.

Then after a short pause that same peculiar, acrid odor was around me again, just like I'd noticed it at the door, but I couldn't tell where it was coming from this time; it was sort of disembodied. Then that drifted away, too, or at least lessened to the point of not being noticeable any more.

I wiped the stickiness from my face and relighted the candle and sat down on the cot to wait for her some more.

It seemed like she'd been gone half the night, but it might have been only three quarters of an hour or so. Then when she did come she was better at it than he had been. I didn't hear her on the stairs at all; just her knock came cautiously through all at once, the way she'd said she'd give it.

I went over and let her in fast. She was loaded down with junk; there were two big bulges under her shawl, one on each side of her, that she was holding up with her arms. She was looking watchfully behind her, to make sure the stairs had stayed empty, when I opened the door. I was surprised at how glad I was to see her; you'd think I'd known her weeks or months already.

She gave me a knowing wink as she brushed by. Meaning: It's okay; everything's under control—or something like that. I refastened the door after her, and she dumped a couple of bundles of stuff on the table where the candle was and thinned out under the lines of the shawl again as a result.

"I found out what you need to know, chico," she began with breathless satisfaction.

"Go easy," I cautioned. "There's somebody right on the other side of the wall here from us."

"Oh, him?" she said unconcernedly. "He's all right. He scares the hell out of you when you first look at him, but he's harmless. He smokes opium, but he minds his own business. He's out of this world half the time; that's why he's a good guy to have in the room right next door to you. I feed him sometimes; otherwise he'd starve to death."

I just gave my collar a stretch and let it go at that. "What luck'd you have?"

She lowered her voice in spite of what she'd just said to me about his other-worldliness. "The picture-postcard shooter that works Sloppy's is called Pepe Campos. He wasn't there any more; he'd called it a night, but I got all the necessary dope on him out of one of the barmen, with the help of a short beer and a little eyelash work. He's got a little hole-in-the-wall room somewhere along Calle Barrios that he uses for a combination studio and sleeping quarters. I couldn't find out the exact house, but it's a short little lane—I know where it is—so that shouldn't give you too much trouble. I also found out something else. This guy I was talking to told me someone else was in there asking for Campos just a little while before I was. Some man."

I didn't like the way that sounded. "It could be just a coincidence. But then again it could be somebody else figured out the same thing I did about his picture plate being the only witness. Two minds with the same thought at the same time, you know. I think I'd better get started fast."

"You'll never make it."

"I've got to make it, Midnight. There's no two ways. All right, you did the groundwork for me; you got me the lead. Now the rest is up to me. I can't just sit here and send out messages by carrier pigeon all night."

She chuckled and swung her elbow at me. "Who you calling a carrier pigeon?" She went over to the table where she'd dumped all the stuff she'd brought in with her and started busting the brown paper apart. "I figured you'd want it that way, so I picked these up for you on my way back at a place I know of."

She took out a not-very-natty outfit consisting of a pair of oil-stained dungarees, a turtle-necked seaman's jumper and a peaked oiler's cap. You could smell the engine room a mile away on all of them.

"Turning me into a wharf rat, are you?"

"It'll give you more of an even chance. At least you won't be spotted on sight if you steer clear of direct overhead street lights. They'd know you were coming, in that stuff you've got on now, from a block away."

"Okay," I said, "turn your back," and I got into them. The odor of machine oil nearly threw you over, but after the first minute or two you got used to it. I wasn't interested in how I smelled right then, anyway.

She scanned me critically when I was through, walked around me in a half circle, cigar tipped up at the alert. "That'll do it," she said finally. "You know, the funny thing about you is, you look more at home in that *embarcadero* rig than in that fancy tourist's outfit you've been sporting until now."

"This is about my speed, I guess."

"Slouch a little when you walk, and those damn-fool cops won't know you for the same guy they lost inside this house, unless they come up and stare you right in the eye. Loosen up your legs a little; that's all you've got to do. A landsman keeps his legs sort of close; a seaman spreads them out for balance. Now listen close. I'm going to give you the directions you've got to take to get from here over to Calle Barrios."

I came in next to her and ducked my head intently.

"I'm not going to give you street names; that'd be just a lot of Greek to you, and you'd only get all tangled up. I'm going to give you just the directions you've got to head in and the number of times you've got to turn. You go down to the mouth of the alley and you turn to the right. That's this hand, here. You follow the street that runs past the alley all the way to its end. When you get to its end, this time you turn left—"

"That's this hand, here," I said dryly.

"Now you're on one of the main stems, and you've got to watch yourself."

She rehearsed me carefully on it. First she ran through it from beginning to end three separate times herself, to get it firmly planted in my mind. Then she made me play it back to her word for word, to make sure I had it, wouldn't go wrong.

"Think you're set now? Havana's a tough town to find your way around in when it's new to you," she warned me.

"I've got it down pat now," I assured her. "I couldn't miss it if I tried."

"Well, just the same, don't try."

"You're a good kid, Midnight," I told her.

"That's something I haven't been called since I was four

years old. And even then they had me mixed up with somebody else."

I dug down deep into the pocket of my old suit. I crammed a fistful of American folding money into her hand, all I had on me. Honeymoon money. "Here," I said. "Just in case something does go wrong and I don't make it. For the outfit—and for being a good scout."

She switched it to the table top and took her hand off it. "I'm not out for money. Not in this, anyway."

This time I said it for her. I was getting to know it by heart. "I know. Flowers on a grave."

"Listen," she assured me jauntily, planing her hand in front of my face, "while there's still a store counter left that I can dip from, or while they still buy my flowers at the café tables and show me where their wallets are while I pin them on for them, don't worry about me; I'll get along. I always have until now."

"You'll never get to heaven."

She shuddered at the very thought. "It must be awfully damn lonely up there, don't you think?"

"All right, if you won't take it, then put it away for me until I get back. And forget where you put it."

I listened toward the stairs, opened the door, and eased past it to the outside. Then I looked around at her before I closed it.

I wasn't any too sure that this wasn't good-by for keeps. I knew I ought to say something, just to sign off, but I didn't know what.

She was standing between me and the candle, so her head was black against the dim glow of it. It made like an aura around her, and she was the last person who ought to have an aura. Or was she?

"Well, be seeing you," I said.

She gave me the Spanish for something; I think it was "Good hunting."

I closed the door behind me.

CHAPTER VII

THE STAIRS WERE ALL right. The only risk there was not putting your foot in the right place and going all the way down them headfirst. I went down them a good deal slower than I'd come up, with them and their light at my heels. I liked this way the better of the two, pitch-dark or not.

Next came the doorway flush with the alley. I eased up to it, back to wall. I evened myself up to the straight line it shaved down across my path, just let my big toe and the turn of my chin and the turn of my nose stick out past it. You couldn't see little things like that in three different places along the wall.

The route down was clear. I couldn't see all the way down to the mouth because of the gloom, but the part from here down was clear; they hadn't left anyone posted. I didn't know what their theory was, but I figured it must be that I'd made my escape good over the roof that time and out through one of the other houses; otherwise they would have left someone hanging up outside the door.

I made the turn of the doorway and started out on the first lap of the long cross-town trip. I swam along close to the wall, and I walked soft. The machine oil still smelled a lot, but then the alley had smelled too, and of the two I liked the smell of the machine oil better.

Of all the outdoor hazards I had ahead of me, this alley stretch right at the beginning was bound to be the toughest, and I was glad it was working out so easy. For one thing, if one of *them* came my way, I couldn't hope to squeeze by without being recognized—there was no room; you practically had to rub noses with anyone trying to pass you. This was the narrowest thing ever; nothing all the rest of the way across town could ever again be this narrow, confine you to such close quarters. And secondly, this was the immediate region in which I'd given them the slip, in which they'd last seen me, and they were likelier to keep a closer watch around here than on any other section I'd pass through on the way over.

Pretty soon the alley mouth lightened up a little ahead of me. Not much, but at least it became the color of pewter or slate, instead of coal-black, from the reflection of the niggardly lights along the lengthwise lane that ran past its foot. I slowed as I got near it and started to pay myself out by hand spans along the wall.

When I'd fitted myself into the corner line again I did the same thing I'd done back at the doorway, let the rough edges of my profile overlap past it.

This time there was a catastrophe.

A voice growled right into my ear—or should I say into my questioning nose, since my ear was still back behind the wall—"*¿Hasta que hora nos quedamos aquí?*"

I thought it was said to me, it was so close and unexpected. I punched my outward shoulder back against the wall in a half turn-around and stayed there as flat as a wet three-sheet that's just been pasted up.

I'd glimpsed the outer edges of his figure, and it wasn't good; it was in police uniform.

I couldn't move for a minute, and before I'd had a chance to the situation bettered itself a trifle. Very little, but at least enough to show that the challenge hadn't been a direct one to me. A second voice answered his: "*Hasta que lo cogimos.*"

So there were a pair of them there, keeping the alley covered. I might have known it was too good to be true. Evidently they'd been silent all along and just made those couple of desultory remarks in time to keep me from stepping around the corner onto their toes. I couldn't understand why she hadn't tipped me off, but maybe they hadn't been here yet when she went out herself; had been posted only after the last time she'd come in.

They didn't say anything more. They were bored at the assignment and not in a conversational mood. Once I heard shoe leather creak as one of them shifted weight. I was afraid even the machine oil would give me away; I was so close to them, even that was a liability. But I guess it had too much else to compete with.

I ebbed back a cautious step, feeling my way behind me with arched foot. Then another. After the third I was a little safer; I turned and went, face forward, in retreat. But very quiet, very tenderly.

I was stuck. Stuck good, and I knew it. There might be an upper outlet to the alley, but if there was and they'd posted men at one end, they'd almost certainly have them posted at the other end too. If they hadn't, they needed to have their heads examined.

Before I could decide what to do about it; in fact, before I'd even recovered the full distance back to my original doorway and that degree of safety at least, the sack I was in closed up even tighter.

There was a tread coming toward me from the recesses of the alley, and when I forced my eyes I could discern movement against the blackness, or rather of it, as a figure sought to detach itself and come forward into visibility. A feat which it could not accomplish, no matter how it narrowed the distance between us; there was not enough light to let it. But someone was astir and bearing down on me, and I was going to be pinned between the two: the lookouts around the corner and this oncoming unknown quantity. There was no break in the walls on either side for me to slip into; it had overspanned the entry to Midnight's house and was already on my side of it, crowding me before it into an everlessening zone of immunity, before I'd discovered it.

I went over to the opposite wall, then back to the first again, in a sort of floundering uncertainty. The difference was only of a pace or two across, and both were equally barren of aid for purposes of evasion. It was a good rattrap to be in. The only thing I didn't do was make the mistake of falling back toward the alley opening again; down there the odds against me were double.

It came on. I'd started forward to meet it now rather than stand still. It seemed to me to have a straggling ring to it that indicated a casual approach rather than an intentional one. In other words, it was coming down this way at random and not because it knew I was there. If I kept going, head low, I might be able to barge past and break through to the other side of it before I was stopped, I figured.

The margin of anonymity between us melted away as we came together, and suddenly we were full abreast, and at another pace I would have been safely to the rear.

It was a girl again. A whiff of sachet in my face and the flirt of a skirt against my leg as I crowded past told me that. This town seemed to be alive with female night prowlers.

Her arm had found the opening under mine—I don't know how—at the instant of passage, and I suddenly found myself locked there in a reversed arm link of companionship, one of us facing one way; the other, the opposite. I would have had to tow her backward after me, full weight, if I'd tried to keep going at that moment.

She said, "*¿Como le va, marinero?*"

I still could hardly see her in the gloom, even with both our elbows entangled. She seemed to be willing to take me sight unseen.

She said something about a drink, I think it was. I got the word *copita*. Did I have the price of a drink, I suppose.

That gave me an idea. I quit trying to wrench her limp arm off mine and let her have it back the long way around, around the back of her own neck. "Okay," I said hurriedly, "you want a drink? Walk close to me like this. . . . No, lean up closer. . . . That's it, snuggle up against me. Now walk down this way with me, just past the corner."

She seemed to have a single phrase of English on tap. Who didn't down there? God knows where she'd picked it up. "You serrit," she said chummily.

"Keep talking," I said. "Keep talking a lot."

"You serrit, you serrit, you serrit," she said obligingly.

I could hardly walk; I was practically carrying her on my right side, she was leaning over so. She had a big celluloid comb arrangement sticking up, and that worked swell; it screened one whole side of my face. The side they were on.

"What do you want, wine or rum?"

"You serrit."

"That's good," I drawled approvingly. "Here's the turn."

We practically took the skin off their faces, we passed them so close. She was on that side, luckily. There were two of them, despondently holding up the wall there. One in cop's uniform, one in mufti.

I was swinging her from side to side as we went by, as though one or both of us had already had more than enough.

She knew them both. She had to show off. Maybe that was good, too, for all I knew.

"Hello," she said airily over her shoulder. "Look what I've got. See?" It sounded as though she stuck her tongue out and gave them the raspberry. They must have been kidding her about slipping, previous to this.

I grinned widely with that side of my face. When I grin, all the skin goes back and folds up. That leaves less face to be inspected. They hadn't been in the original party in the car, anyway.

We were well past them now, doing a slow sway from side to side.

They hollered out something after us about *dientes.* I think it was meant for me. To hang onto my gold teeth, probably.

I kept her with me until we got as far as I was going on the transverse. Then all of a sudden she had nothing but air around her, and it kept getting wider every minute.

"See you some more," I said, and pitched my thumb back the way we'd just come.

She wasn't one-phrase in Spanish, whatever she was in English. She sent up a shower of epithets that rained down all over, from one end of the block to the other. It reminded me of a water main bursting in the street behind me. Only one carrying vocabulary instead of water.

"You serrit," I palmed back at her.

The last I saw of her she was scurrying actively around, looking for handy stones to throw after me, but fortunately there weren't any of a size that mattered lying around loose.

I joined up with one of the main arteries soon after that, and I had to watch myself. Conditions had reversed themselves, from what they'd been back there in the alley and the lanes around it; there were too many lights now instead of too few. Every thirty yards or so one of these multiple electric lampposts would show up, bearing five warm golden globes instead of just one and bleaching the sidewalk all around it like full-strength daytime sunshine. True, they alternated from side to side of the way, but I couldn't keep crossing back and forth just to avoid them; that would have been even more of a giveaway.

There were cafés along this street, too, open to the street, with tables paid out along the sidewalk and sending out a calcium glare that made everything stand out like high noon. I had to skirt them as best I could, pretending to look the other way, or pretending to scratch my head so I could get my arm up on that side. For all I knew, one of *them* might be sitting down there on one of those spidery little iron chairs, staring straight out at me. It was like being on exhibition in the line-up; only you kept going instead of standing still. One thing I found out during this half-hour or so—and to me it wasn't a point in its favor—and that's that Havana is a town that never sleeps. They say New York is that way, but New York is a ten o'clock town by comparison. It takes the tropics to show you what real wakefulness in the early hours of the morning is. And I didn't want to be shown right then.

Then when there weren't cafés to buck, and I'd get a nice comparatively overcast stretch just ahead, a trolley car would come banging down on me—they ran there right in the middle—shedding turquoise sparks from its overhead traction wire and casting a livid, rippling wash along the walls from its ceiling lights. They were open, too, sideless, with the benches on them running crosswise; they were packed to the gills whenever they did show up, and there were all those rows of faces staring woodenly at you for a minute or two, while you were held impaled there in the bright backwash it threw up. At least that was what it felt like to me.

I couldn't get off the damned thoroughfare either and try my luck with some quieter alternate farther over. Her instructions were rigid and didn't allow for substitutions; they were complicated enough and hard to keep straight as it was, and I was afraid if I took any detours I'd get all tangled up, never be able to get back on course again. This town wasn't laid out in rectangles like Miami; the streets were all hit or miss, like the cracks in a picture puzzle.

Well, I made it. There weren't any shouts of recognition and there wasn't any sudden stampede after me, so I considered that I'd made it. I came to this white marble statue that she'd told me to keep my eyes out for—some patriot or other; I couldn't remember the name—and I turned off there, like she'd coached me to. From this point on it got better, dimmer again. I was safely on the other side of "downtown" now, opposite the one from which I'd started, and getting farther away from the feverish heart of the town all the time. Streets were cool and blue-dark again with night shadows, and the people you passed on them fewer and fewer all the time.

It was a long trek, and I kept giving my memory refresher courses in it as I went along, to make sure of not going wrong. I've never been book-smart and I've never been clever, but I've always had a good mechanical memory. Once you pound a thing into it often enough, it hangs onto it tight. She hadn't burdened me with street names; that would have been hopeless. I couldn't even pronounce half of them myself the first time, much less store them up ahead. She'd just given me the arithmetical factors of direction, with landmarks to break them up.

The night was hot. The breeze blowing up some of the streets from the harbor fooled you at times, but it was hot, and all that walking in it brought the sweat out. My mongrel attire itched, and my legs ached from the unaccustomed spread gait at which I held them distorted.

I got there finally. I passed the little movie house that was the last of all the landmarks she'd given to me; dark and dead to the world at this hour, with a sign over it, "Cine," and big tattered posters feathering the walls all around the entrance. Some ancient forgotten film still grinding away here in the byways of the town years after all the rest of the world had seen it: "Fred Astaire en Volando Hasta Rio." I made the turn it fronted on, and I'd hit it. Calle Barrios.

A little one-block affair with shedlike arrangements on supports roofing over a good deal of its sidewalks, so that they were in even deeper shadow than those elsewhere. She hadn't been able to give me the exact house—her informant at Sloppy's evidently hadn't known that himself—so from this point on I was strictly on my own.

I moved slowly from doorway to doorway, paling them one side at a time with flickering palm-enclosed matches, looking for some placard or other indication. He was a professional photographer, so I figured he must have some way of advertising himself down below at the street door, to give people a tumble that he was up there.

I got plenty, but not what I was looking for. I got a dentist, I got a *licenciado*—whatever that was—I got a woman who sewed or made dresses or something. I even got a guy who changed foreign money for you; I bet he gypped you plenty, too, if you were fool enough to go near him. I got to the end of the block on that side of the street. I ran out of doorways.

I crossed over to the opposite side and started to work my way back along there. Once I had to stop, a guy was coming along the sidewalk, not on my side but across the way, and I had to wait until he went past. I thought that maybe that match-fluttering act might make him suspicious, or at least nosy. He didn't see me standing there under the gloom of the overhanging sidewalk shed. He came along whistling. He went straight through the street and turned off again at the other end. I could still hear his whistling a minute or two after that in the heavy quiet, and then it faded away. I sort of envied him, whoever he was. He hadn't had his lady killed tonight. He didn't have to hide out along the streets. He could go home whistling.

I shrugged and struck a new match and started in again. It came right on with the flowering of the flame, as though it had been waiting there all along, right under my hand, to be revealed to me. "Campos. Retratos y Fotografías." I recognized him by the name she'd given me, and then the last word would have told me anyway. It was the same as ours, only spelled a little different. And then there was a picture of a hand under it, pointing inward to show that was the doorway that was meant, and not any other. Which struck me as being a little superfluous, but every man to his own taste. And then there was a small 3 under it to show the floor.

I blew out the match and I went in.

They didn't believe in wasting lights by leaving them on all night. You were supposed to be in by now if you belonged here, I suppose. I groped until I found stairs, and then I felt my way painfully up them. I counted out two landings, and then when the next one came I knew that was where I got off. As a matter of fact, it was the last one anyway.

I went back to matches again to make sure of getting the right door. There was no difficulty about that. There were only two in sight, and one of them didn't belong to anybody. It was the door to a water closet. I proved that by looking, but you could have told without even opening it, anyway. I went back to the other door, braced myself, and knocked subduedly.

I thought: How am I going to make him understand me? He might know a word or two of English; most of them down here seemed to. I tried to remember whether he'd used any in accosting the two of us at Sloppy's, but I couldn't any more. Too much had happened since.

He must be asleep long ago. I knocked again, a little less tactfully.

Money would do it. Money talks in any language. But I didn't have any. I'd left my roll with Midnight. Well, all else failing, I had a pair of persuaders down at the end of my arms. If I couldn't talk to him—and I had no money that could talk to him—they'd have to talk to him. But I'd only use them as a language of last resort.

I hadn't been able to rouse him yet. I pummeled good and loud this time. And waited. And still he didn't come. I tried the door, but that was too much to hope for, that I'd just be able to walk in like that, at will.

I pounded some more. This time I hit it on all cylinders. It went rolling down through the slumbering house, hollow and distorted, like thunder that had strayed in some way and was trying to find its way out again. Then it tapered off, but only long after I'd quit knocking.

A door opened somewhere down below, and a woman shouted up shrilly: "*¡Cállese!*" Shut up up there, I suppose. Then she waited, to see if I was going to do it again. I wasn't and I didn't. If he'd been in there he would have heard me by now. She slammed inside again finally, simmering to herself.

I gave her a minute or two to go back to sleep. Then I struck a match and examined the door. I wasn't going to give up. I hadn't come all the way across Havana to turn around and go away again, no better off than I had been before.

It had a transom over it of dust-pearled glass. It wasn't down quite flat; it was teetered in about a quarter of an inch out of its frame. But the thing was, it wasn't a fixed panel, a fanlight. If it went up a quarter of an inch, it could be made to go up farther than that. It must be moveable, must work on a hinge or rod of some sort.

Scott was going to get in there.

I aimed for the bottom of its frame with the heels of both my hands, sprang for it, missed getting a fast enough hold, and dropped back again. I aimed again, sprang again, this time caught on and swayed there. I got my foot on the doorknob, and that gave me a brace. I nudged into the panel with my shoulder, and it moved quite easily, almost flapped back loosely. The hinge must have been broken. It came back each time, but that didn't matter; at least it didn't stick.

I got my head down in through it and was looking at the dark upside down. Then I worked one shoulder and arm through and let myself go farther. I was afraid to let go altogether and just drop. I would have landed headfirst and might have knocked myself out. More important, the crash might bring up someone from the floor below to investigate.

I located the inside knob with one acutely downstretched arm and then found a cross-latch just above it. In tight, so he must still be in there, because that sort of latch could be worked only from the inside. I felt like a clothespin, with my rump riding the transom. I slipped the latch grip over and then had to work myself back outside again. Which wasn't as easy as getting in. Once I thought I wasn't going to make it and would have to hang there suspended the rest of the night. The back of my head kept hitting the transom and closing it down on my own neck.

I finally got out again and dropped down to the floor outside and then went in the way you're supposed to through any door, head uppermost and feet to the ground.

It reminded me a little of when I'd busted into Midnight's room an hour or two back—or was it a year ago now? Only this was even darker. There wasn't even a red cigarette glint this time. It was like being tangled up on the wrong side of a heavy black velvet curtain and trying to cuff your way out through it. Except that you couldn't feel velvet folds in front of you; you could just feel plain black air.

I thought: He's got to be here because the latch was shot home on the inside of the door. And yet how could he be and still fail to hear that drubbing I'd given the door?

I was going to light a match first, but then I realized that wouldn't show me much; it would only show him me, if he was here. If his work was photography, even third-rate photography, there must be electricity in the place. I turned and started to measure off the wall alongside the doorframe, hand over hand. When I'd gone up about as high as my shoulder I quit and did it on the other side. There wasn't anything on either side.

I started forward a few paces, trying to get to room center, so I'd be able to get my match's worth, as long as I had to use one. I think I had about two left by this time out of the whole double fistful I'd brought away from Midnight's place.

All of a sudden something tickled the rim of my ear. I thought it was a mosquito or gnat for a minute and swerved my head, but then it came back on the other side. I clawed out in a sort of stifled fright, and something pulled tight across the edge of my hand, caught, and then clicked at the other end. The light I'd been looking for went on straight over my head, in a sort of blinding cascade, and I was holding the other end of the dangling string that worked it.

I couldn't use my eyes for a minute after so much darkness. Then I took the back of my hand away, and they went to work again.

I didn't like what I saw.

CHAPTER VIII

IT WAS JUST A small attic room, about what you'd expect for a shoestring-photographer's studio. It had no windows, but the ceiling broke in the middle; on one side of this central seam it was level and at full room height; on the other it sloped downward in a sort of gable effect, and the end wall was only about shoulder-high. In this sloped section there was a skylight vent. That was one of the things I didn't like the looks of.

It had been glassed over, but the glass was all out, except for a spiny fringe around the edges, and you could see stars needling the black up above it. Directly underneath the gap the floor was all twinkling and littered with shards of broken glass. That meant unlawful entry. Then there was a straight-backed chair standing there in position right under the rent, and that meant unlawful exit again. It had been moved over after the glass had already fallen through, because its seat was clean; there were no particles a-twinkle on it such as even a brushing off would have left.

It was easy enough to read the little still life. Somebody had jumped down through the skylight, feet first. Somebody had climbed up out through it again, using the chair for a stepladder.

It looked like there had been a fight, or at least some kind of strenuous resistance, in between the two events. Two other chairs like the first that he'd had in there were lying toppled flat on their backs, and a couple of the legs of one were badly fractured. The portable tripod he carried around with him was lying there on the floor, smashed, and with all its guts spilled out, as though somebody had been trying to wrench it apart in a hurry to get the plates out, or it had been plentifully stepped on in the course of a struggle.

A couple of sample portraits that he'd had tacked on the walls as a decoration had slipped their moorings, jarred out of true by the vibration. One had dropped down all the way; the other still clung tenuously by one corner.

That about finished the front room, or at least the main part of it, that he'd used for posing his subjects. There was, however, a curtain strung across one entire side of it, to my left as I came in, subdividing the already modest space into two unequal parts. It had, strangely enough, not been disturbed, or, if it had, had fallen back into proper place again without revealing any trace of it.

I went over to it, jerked it aside, and looked through. Behind it there was just an alcove, a small rectangle that he used as a combination darkroom, for developing his plates, and sleeping quarters. There was a cot crowded into it, and then there was an ordinary built-in washbasin against the wall that he used for a developing tank. It was still full of solution, but there were no pictures soaking in it when I stuck my hand in and felt carefully all around the sides and bottom.

He had a wire strung diagonally across the tiny cubicle, from curtain pole to wall, that he'd used for hanging negatives on to dry, like wash on a line, but they'd all been pulled off by somebody, as if in hasty examination, and then thrown down. They lay all over the floor, like curled-up black celluloid leaves.

I didn't bother retrieving them and taking them out into the light and going over them individually to see if the one I wanted was among them. I didn't have to. There was a short cut to finding that out. I counted up the negatives at sight from where I stood: there were eight lying around me. Then I counted up the "clothespins," the little wooden grips he'd used to fasten them with, that were still hooked onto the line. There were nine. One negative had gone out of here—up through the skylight.

So had he. The cot had been slept in; it was easy to see that. The lower end of the coverings still retained the funnel shape his legs had hollowed out in them; the upper end had been ravaged, violently cast asunder, as if by a startled leap to upright position. At the sound of glass sundering and spilling down into the room on the other side of the curtain, most likely.

He hadn't had time to dress. His coat and shirt and tie were lying on the floor, all mangled and stepped over. They must have taken him with them just as he was. Or at least just lingered long enough to force his kicking legs into pants and shoes and then hoisted him out with them the same way they'd come in. There was no sign of these last two items anywhere around.

He hadn't gone docilely. The condition of the outside part of the room showed there must have been quite an unheaval, a weighted staggering back and forth and flinging around, before he'd gone at all. Then maybe when he had at last, he'd gone out senseless, they'd had to do it that way. In here, to show for it, there was a little slap of blood on one of the sheets that lay trailing off the cot toward the curtain, as though caught around someone's foot. I pressed my thumb down on it, and the linen was soggy yet there where it was. Just now. Just a little while before I got here, maybe after I was already well on the way over. Just a little too soon. Good timing. But not for me.

Well, he hadn't gone submissively. I gave him credit for that much, anyway.

I went out slow, even slower than I'd gone in, and I'd certainly made my way in slowly enough. I reached back over my shoulder and gave the light cord a disgusted tweak as I drifted by below it, and the room went back into the oblivion it had been in before I came here. Just a glimpse in the night of a strange room in a strange town. Someplace you'd never seen before and would never see again. And yet the memory of it would probably stay with me far longer than of many another far more familiar place.

There went my last chance. I elbowed the door closed behind me and teetered through the dark toward the place where I last remembered leaving the stairs.

CHAPTER IX

ALL THE WAY BACK across town I kept wondering why I was bothering to make the trip back at all. Why annoy her any more? I didn't have any claim on her. She'd done enough for me already. More than once, especially when I'd come to elbows or bends, when my course would change directions, I was tempted to just keep straying on at random and not bother with my memorized road map any more. Especially when I cut across streets that I could tell led straight down to the waterfront. It's funny how water, or rather its margins, always attracts you when you're at a loss, don't know what to do or where to go next. Something about it.

I kept away, though. It wouldn't have been a good place for me. They know that about it too. They expect you to do that. They were probably keeping watch down there along the docks and loading platforms.

So I kept to my course, in reverse. It didn't seem nearly as arduous as the first time, nor nearly as risky. Perhaps that was because I'd already covered it once, and familiarity breeds contempt. Or perhaps I was more indifferent than I had been coming out, didn't care so much whether I made it or not any more. I was already licked and just needed to be pushed down to stay down. You have to go somewhere, so I went back toward where I'd started from.

A lot of the bloom had been taken off the cafés; they weren't as bad this time. It was getting late, even for an all-night town. Several were dark now, and several more were dimmed down to the extinction point, tables being stacked back to back. The trolleys didn't hound me any more the way they had, either; they'd either stopped or were running on a slower schedule.

Once a prosperous-looking colored man in a natty white suit came up to me in the gloom and asked me something. It was legitimate, whatever it was; I could tell that by his aboveboard manner, but I couldn't get it. Standing there, he looked like something printed on a photographic negative—I guess I had pictures on my mind after what had just happened—but he was all white where he should have been black, and all black where he should have been white. He repeated himself twice, then at my "Don't know what you're saying" gave me up as hopeless and went on to try the next person, if any, to be found at that hour. He might have just wanted a light, for all I know, but I wasn't lighting up my face for anyone. That was the only thing that happened the whole way back.

They weren't on duty at the alley mouth any more; they'd been called off. I could tell the way was clear from all the way back at the outermost limits of visibility, which wasn't such a great distance at that; the walls were evenly toned there where it opened, no dark spots against them. They might, of course, have shifted around the corner to the inside, but I doubted that. A cop usually stays where you first find him, so long as he doesn't know you've found him there.

I turned the corner and went in myself, and there was no one on the inside of it either. They'd given up and called off the chase, at least for the present.

The rest was easy. I found my way in and up the stairs, and I knocked the same way she had when she'd come back before, so she'd know that it was me. She took a minute or two—but you couldn't hear her—and then she opened it up, and there we both were, right back where we'd started again.

I guess she could tell by the look on my face and the boneless way I was propped there against the doorframe, before she even asked me anything.

"Mala suerte, huh?" she grunted.

"If you mean no good, that's it." I thumbed my cap visor still farther up on my head. Otherwise I didn't move.

"Well, come in, don't stand there; what're you waiting for—the rainy season to end?"

"What'll I do inside?"

"Well, what'll you do outside?"

I moved a little sluggishly, and she got the door fastened up behind me.

"Somebody beat me to it," I said disgustedly. "They not only took the picture, but they took him with it."

"*Carajo,*" she breathed sympathetically.

"You can say that again, once for me, whatever it is. It proves one thing, even if nothing else," I told her. "Something *did* show up on that picture, and there would have been an out for me in it, or they wouldn't have gone to all that trouble just to get hold of it. They hijacked him along with it to shut him up because he'd already developed it and seen what was on it for himself. Otherwise they would have just knocked him out and left him there. It's developed on the film now and it's also developed on his mind; that's why they had to take the two things with them. Too bad I didn't get the idea an hour sooner; I could have gotten in under the wire."

I gave her a turn of the arm and reached for the door again, to go back downstairs where I'd just come from.

She grabbed me and held me fast. "You're not quitting, are you?"

"What do you want me to do? I can't camp out up here in your place for the rest of my life, set up light housekeeping between flying raids from the police."

"What's the matter? You afraid it won't be respectable?" she peered. "It's only safe, middle-class people that never were on the run in their lives that think a man and a woman can't stay in the same room overnight without getting tangled up with one another. Us underdogs know better. I was holed up in a room with a guy for thirty solid days once in New Orleans—neither one of us could get out—and I bet we were more proper than half these rich families that live out on the Vedado in thirty-room mansions. We were too busy watching for the police to think of watching each other dressing. There's a cot here and there's a floor; what more do we need? There's just two of us."

She jogged me over toward the cot, to have a seat on it. I had a seat on it.

"At least ride the night out here."

"It'll take a year of nights, and then some. What chance have I got of clearing myself now?"

She came over and looked down at me. "I see I've got to talk to you to get it into your head. You *chamacos* from up North, you don't seem to think in a straight line like we do; you go around curves." She pummeled me encouragingly on the chest with the back of her hand a couple of times. "You've still got a chance; that hasn't changed any. You've still got the same chance you had before, when you started out to get that picture. Only now, instead of getting just the picture back, you've got to get a whole live photographer."

"Sure, a cinch," I said glumly.

She made with her hands. "Well, which is easier to track down and spot—a complete man-size guy or a little two-by-four picture that can be stuck away in anyone's pocket? Don't you see, hombre, they've given themselves away to you?

"You know now, by their taking him off like that, that he knows something that could help you, that he saw something on that negative when he developed it. You've got more now than you had before."

"I'm loaded down with it," I assented parenthetically.

"Now you're sure; before you weren't. It's just as good as if you saw the picture yourself."

Her line of reasoning was okay as far as it went, but I couldn't follow it through, get what she was driving at.

"All right, *I* know. But the police don't know. I'm not hard to convince; I never did think I was guilty. They're the ones need the telling, not me."

"But I know how you can get these others to tell the police on themselves, just as they told you. It's a very slim chance. It all depends on whether you are willing to gamble ten to one against your own life."

I gave a short laugh. "I'd be willing to take even longer odds than that. Twenty to one. Twenty-five. What kind of odds am I up against now? You don't call them short, do you? And what's so valuable about the damn thing to me now, with *her* out of the way, anyway? I don't have to save it for a rainy day."

She bore down on my shoulder, as a sign of approval, I suppose. "That's right, chico. That's the talk. You've got the right idea."

"What's this angle that you've got? Let's hear it."

"Here's what it is, here. Simply to let them get you as they got the photographer. You know who I mean by *them,* don't you? This bunch, this outfit, or whoever they are. Fall into their hands. Only it must seem accidental, not on purpose."

"I don't catch. Then they'll turn me over to the police right away, and that's what I've been dodging all night long."

"No, they won't. Don't you see, *hijo,* now they can't any more. They daren't. You know what happened to this photographer now: that he was grabbed off to keep him quiet. You can prove there was such a guy and there isn't now any more in circulation. Nobody can get around that; you didn't just make him up out of thin air. He existed. And now where is he? All right. So even though you still can't clear yourself of the other thing, you *can* pin that on them. And they know it, you bet. If you let yourself fall conveniently into their hands the police will never see you. Not alive, not able to talk." She spun an imaginary grain of dust off my shoulder with a snap of her finger. "You follow me so far?"

"Sure. Up to the point where I'm dead instead of alive, but that isn't such a hot solution. For that matter, I could cut my throat right here in this room; that would be even quicker still."

She pressed down the air with the flats of her hands in a soft-pedaling motion. "Now wait a minute. Don't muddy it up. *Mira.* They can't let the photographer go because he'll tell the police about the picture. They can't let you go—once they have you—because you'll tell the police about the photographer." She spread her hands. *"Claro,* no?"

"Claro, yes," I admitted, picking up the word for whatever it was worth. "But what makes you think the photographer is still alive? If your point is that once they get me I'll be a dead duck, doesn't that hold equally true of him? They have the same reason in both cases."

"He's still alive up to now. The fact that they didn't finish him off right there at his *estudio* is proof enough of that. Why should they carry a dead body off with them, especially the hard way, up through a skylight and down off a roof? They'd just give it to him otherwise and leave him behind." She made a slashing motion across her own throat. "He was still alive when they took him with them. How long he's going to stay that way, that's another matter. They either intend to get rid of him out of town someplace, where his remains will not be discovered so quickly, or in the ocean, where they will not be discovered at all."

"And I suppose if I drop into their laps that's what will happen to me? Is that your setup?" I gave her an off-center grin.

"That's only Part One of my setup. Part Two has to follow immediately, like they say in the *cines*. If it doesn't, then it's just too bad for you. That's your one chance out of the ten that I spoke of before. Part One is, you fall into their hands and they start the job of finishing you off. Part Two is, you and they both—the whole mess of you—fall into the hands of the police, and they finish the whole thing off for everybody. Well, all right, the guilt speaks for itself; they don't have to use their magnifying glasses. Who was kidnaping who? Who was trying to shut up who? Were you trying to rub them out, or were they trying to rub you out? They've got two strikes against them, like we used to say in Tampa. You and the photographer. When they're trying to shut so many people up, then they've got something to shut them up about. You haven't; you're not trying to. *¿Como te parece?* What do you think of it; it's a good scheme, no?"

"It's lovely. I'd like to do something like it every Tuesday evening about nine or quarter past."

She flung up her hand high overhead in reproach. "It's the only one we got, isn't it? What're you talking about? You got a better one, spit it out!"

"It's the only one we got," I said wearily, "so it goes. And don't get me wrong; I'm not kicking." I stood up from the cot and gave my dungarees a hoist back and front. "I'm still willing to take the one chance left over out of those ten; that's good enough for me. I'd take it if it was one out of fifty. But the thing is, will it work? You've just given it a beating with your gums, and it comes out swell. But can it be turned into action?"

"Why can't it?" she snapped at me.

"Let's begin at the beginning. This is going to take all night. All right, first off I fall into their hands; that's the starter. Now will you tell me how the holy hell I'm going to fall into their hands when I don't even know *who* they are, or *where* they are, or how to *go* where they are so I *can* fall into their hands? What do you expect me to do—walk around all night with a sandwich board on my chest: 'I'm waiting for you guys to grab me?' "

"Don't get so funny." She squelched me inattentively, running a fingernail up and down between two of her teeth in perplexed abstraction.

"I wouldn't even know them if I saw them," I grumbled. "They could be anybody at all."

"Shut up." She spit out the small end of a cigar and bent over the candle with it, sucking in flame. "Anything that can be put together can be taken apart again. This frame was nailed together around you; we can find the joints, take it apart into little separate pieces again, if we only keep at it long enough."

"What d'ya say we do?" I assented dourly.

"That fat Chinaman is in on it in some way, that Tío Chin. That much you can be sure of. All the trouble started from his place. You and she were purposely steered there; he palmed the wrong knife off on you, faked the receipt, framed you to the police."

"Him I would like to kick the wind out of." I nodded darkly. "And I don't know why I've hung around here this long without going back there and letting some air out of that balloon-belly of his."

"Hold it," she said, and hauled me back. "Just busting in that store of his and beating him up won't do you any good. You won't find out any more than you know now. He'll squeal like a stuck pig; the cops'll come down on you again, and you'll be right back where you started from. The spiked evidence of the knife and the receipt and all the rest of it will still hold good."

"But you're going against your own argument, aren't you? You just finished saying that they'll grab me, that they can't afford to turn me over to the police now any more."

"Sure, but you've got to put yourself in the right position for them to grab you. They're only going to grab you if they think you're not expecting it; you don't know who they are; you're not wise to them. They're not going to grab you if you go busting in that store the front way, beat him up; they'll know you're wise to him. Besides, this Chin isn't alone in it. He's just the front for somebody else. He never saw you before in his life, so what did he get out of framing you up? There's somebody behind him."

"That's easy. That takes it all the way back to Florida. If this Chin is in on it with somebody else, if there's somebody behind him, like you say, he must be working for Eddie Roman in some way."

"That's what we've got to figure out, the link between the two of them. That'll show us where the two pieces fit together; that'll show us the place for you to squeeze yourself in, so we can be sure they'll grab you."

I pushed the peak of my cap farther back on my forehead. "Now what would a big shot 'sport' and nightclub operator in Florida want with a Chinese agent in Havana? Chin deals in curios and antiques down here. Roman has no use for anything like that in any of his clubs. Not even in his own house; it was all shiny and modernistic. Yet there must be some form of transaction between them."

"You used to do his driving for him. Didn't you ever catch onto what his real business, his real source of income was?"

"Only what met the eye. Nightclubs, races, stuff like that."

"That's a short season down there. Did he go up North when his clubs closed down, operate someplace else?"

"No, he stayed there all year round."

"Then he didn't live off nightclubs. Nine months in the year, where was his money coming from?"

"I don't know," I admitted. "That was stuff that went

on inside the house. I was outside it, sitting behind the wheel most of the time, don't forget."

"She was inside it. She was married to him. Didn't she ever tell you anything?"

"She didn't know any more than I did. She got it in the form of diamonds, but what shape it was in before it got turned into diamonds, I don't think she knew herself."

"That wouldn't have been me, boy. Get something on everyone; that's my motto."

"He was too cagey."

"She must have dropped some little remark or other, even if she didn't know what it was herself. Any woman tells the guy she loves all about the guy she doesn't love any more; that's female instinct. Try to think, will you? Some morning when she got in the car alone with you. It's right there—it must be—if you can only remember it."

I thought back and thought back to a hundred dead and gone mornings, when we went speeding out the driveway, until we could get far enough away to exchange our first kiss unseen. Suddenly a word came to me. Came back to me from one of them. I flexed a finger at her. "What's guava?" I asked her.

"What about it? Let's hear it."

"I asked you first."

"It's a fruit paste. Solid, rubbery sort of stuff."

"She said something about that once. She asked *me,* just like I'm asking you now, but I couldn't tell her. She overheard something one night, and she told me about it the next day in the car. You know, we used to park and then sit there together by the hour."

She wasn't interested in the mechanics of our love affair. "*Por supuesto*. But go ahead."

"And she'd tell me every little thing that had happened since the last time, since the day before, or two days before, or whenever it was. And this was one of those little things. It wasn't anything. It came at the tail end of everything else, just to have something more to say to me."

She made avaricious grasping motions with both hands. "Well, let's hear it, anyway; let's see what it is."

"Give me a minute now to see if I can fish it up in one piece. The phone rang one night and woke her. Four in the morning—some ungodly hour like that. It was right there by their bed. It was for him, of course. Well, he picked it up, and then she heard him say, 'Hold it a second; I'll talk to you from downstairs.' And then he went to all the trouble of putting on robe and slippers, going down to the first floor, and taking the call from there, when he could have stayed just where he was in the first place. The scratchy noises coming from the open receiver bothered her and, half asleep as she was, she reached over to put it back on and shut it up, as long as he didn't need it any more up there where she was. She put it to her ear for a minute to make sure he was on below, and that was how she got a snatch of this conversation. This business conversation. And the only thing that struck her strange about it was the peculiar hour."

"She heard some of it?"

"Just a little. He was talking to some man, evidently someone who worked for him, and the man said: 'But, boss, I can't keep the launch cruising around in circles all night. I had to unload it somewhere.'

"Roman cursed him out and was sore at some delay. She heard him say, 'Why didn't you land it yesterday, when you were expected to? You've tied everything up in a knot. Now I'll have to send a truck down to that Godforsaken place all over again to pick it up.'

"The man said, 'We couldn't help it; there was a hitch at the other end.'

"Roman thought for a minute, then she heard him say, 'Well, as long as it's already unloaded, stay there with it where you are. I'll have the truck down as soon after daylight as I can. How many cases of the guava are there?'

"She heard the man say, 'Five dozen; three and two.' And that was about all she listened to. She hung up and went back to sleep. She mentioned it to me in passing, but it didn't add up; neither of us could figure out what was behind it."

"To me it sounds very much like smuggling."

I nodded. "A launch. Some lonely spot on the beach at night. Then he sends a truck down to pick it up, whatever it is. What does this guava look like; how does it come?"

"You can see it in all the grocery stores here; it's a standard confection. They pack it in layers, in cigar-sized plywood boxes, about so." She shaped her hands about an oblong. "And not more than a couple of inches deep, as a rule."

"I don't get it. Those clubs of his—there was no outlet for it there."

"There's no duty on it, no reason to smuggle it in. It was something more than just guava."

"Yeah, but what? I thought at the time that maybe it was rum or something that he was trying to beat the Federal tax on. That was before I knew how this stuff was packaged. But rum would have to come in barrels; it couldn't come in little flat thin slabs.

"About ten days later," I added inconsequentially, "he gave her a walloping diamond bracelet, a regular sling for a broken wing. Whether it had any connection with that phone call or not, I don't know. She yanked it off, I remember, and nearly skinned her arm raw, and threw it on the back seat and spit after it, while she was sitting there in the front with me."

"So there was a big return on the stuff, whatever it was. It paid off better than rum or anything else, if he could do that. Keep at it, keep with it, see if we can get it."

I don't know how long we sat trying to puzzle it out. I haven't got much imagination. I'd thought of rum, and I couldn't seem to get much past that. What they used to call white slavery cropped up in my mind once, but I junked that; it wouldn't fit in with small cigar-sized boxes.

The place smelled bad, and I shook my head to try to keep it clear for the job we'd picked out. I wrinkled my nose at her. "Gee, it stinks in here. What is that?"

It was the same acrid odor that had bothered me before while she was out and I was waiting for her, alone. It seemed to have come back again, or else it was still hanging around. A little bit like burned feathers, a little bit like sour dough.

"Oh, that's *him* inside there. Don't pay any attention to that." She thumbed the wall behind her back, the dividing one between this room and the next. Something that sounded like the low-voiced groan of a sleeper tossing in distress came through in the moment of silence that followed. Then a soft thud, then nothing. "He probably just came to and lit up again. That goes on off and on all—"

She shut up abruptly, looked at me. I looked at her. We both got it together, in one of those sudden flashes that sometimes strike two people at one and the same time.

"That's it!" she said, and gave her fingers a snap. I knew what she meant.

"Opium! Raw opium embedded in the guava! Probably between the two layers of it, in those little flyweight boxes you told me about. There's his source of income! Not the clubs and tracks up there. A thousand percent profit on every nugget. Ten thousand percent."

"There's the tie-up with Chin. Chin imports antiques and curios, jars and vases and fancy boxes from the East. I bet half of them with fake bottoms. Then he reships from here. This is a way station. It doesn't come from here. But it's a lot easier to get it in from here than it would be straight over from China. They keep a closer watch for it from that direction. Chin's the—how do you say it in English—?"

"The middleman." I was thinking of *her,* though. No wonder she'd hated those jewels he'd showered on her. No wonder she'd wanted to drop them overside into the water, right tonight when we were coming ashore. She hadn't known; I was sure of that. But her instinct had told her there was something about them; it must have, for her to loathe them so. I remembered how she'd said they'd spoken to her at night in the dark, from the dresser top in funny, squeaky, piping voices. The voices of lost souls going down into hell.

I took my hand away from my eyes, uncovered them. She'd stopped for a moment, short of the door, on her way out. She dipped, hiked up the bottom of her skirt so suddenly, I thought she was going to take it off altogether for a minute. She fumbled with the top of her stocking, let the skirt drop again. "And now I know of some good use for that money you tried to wish on me before!"

I saw where she was going, knew what she was going to try to do with it. "Can they talk to you when they're that way? Can they understand you? Can they tell you anything?"

She flourished my own wad of bills at me. "*This* talks, even in nightmares. I'm bringing him a handful of new dreams, aren't I? And maybe even a new fellow customer to share his dreams with him!"

CHAPTER X

SHE WAS IN THERE a long time. She had a hard time with him. I don't know how she did it. She seemed to know how to do it, though. Bring them down to earth again from the poppy clouds they float around in high up above. Maybe she'd had to do it before at one time or another. Or maybe it was just her instinct and practical common sense that told her what to do. Just like a woman in the upper sunlit regions will know how to nurse someone who is ill, intuitively, without ever having taken a nurse's training, so she, down here in the shadowy underworld, seemed to know how to cope with an opium fiend without ever having been tainted by addiction herself.

I could hear her intermittently through the wall while the process went on, and it made my blood run cold at times with sheer reflex horror. Not that the telltale sounds in themselves were horrifying—they were commonplace enough—it was knowing what the basis of the situation was that made my stomach turn.

Her voice reached me by itself at first, unaccompanied, monotonous, insistent, saying the same thing over and over. It would stop, then it would go on again. Perhaps close to his ear. I quickly blinked that thought out of my mind as the memory of what he had looked like returned to me. One phrase, over and over, until you wanted to go nuts and grab hold of the top of your head, even though you were a room away. Maybe "Wake up," or maybe "Talk to me," or maybe just calling him by his name; I don't know what it was.

Then I heard a tin gasoline can clonk once on the floor and the splash water made being poured from it into some smaller receptacle. She must have found some way of heating it; perhaps he had a small alcohol stove in there. This took awhile. And meanwhile the voice went on, mechanical, like a record when the needle is stuck in one place. Then the water again, sloshing more softly this time, as though some rag or other were being saturated in it. Then a sodden, slapping sound, as though someone were being belabored with an improvised hot towel.

A groaning and eerie whimper now underscored her voice when it sounded. Then she seemed to lose him again; he must have slipped back into oblivion. There was a thud, as of someone falling prone from a semi-erect position.

My heart thudded with him.

The slapping became sharper, like a whipcrack; it wasn't with a saturated cloth now; it was with the flat of the hand.

Suddenly everything stopped and she'd come back to our own room. The door flapped open and she was standing in it, breathless, her forehead sequined with moisture, a strand of her hair down out of place over one eye.

"I nearly had him! Then he got away from me again! Quick, give me one of your cigarettes!"

I didn't get it; I was slow on the pickup. Like a dope, I thought for a minute she wanted it for herself. She grabbed it from me, jerked it into her mouth, bent over the candle for a moment, and then beat it back there again, leaving a little bluish haze in the air where she'd been standing.

I got what she'd really wanted it for only after she was already gone again. She never smoked those things herself —she'd told me so—she was a cigar smoker. But I guess there's too big a coal on a cigar.

"I'm going nuts if I get much more of those sound effects," I told myself, and walked around a lot in tight corkscrew circles that kept getting smaller each time around, until they ended in standing still in one place.

The yelp was loud and clear when it came, and it blew all the fog away. I tried not to picture it, but I couldn't help wondering how deep she'd had to go, how long she'd had to—hold it steady.

That did it; that ended it. After that there were just the two voices, murmuring low.

That part of it took a long time too. I guess she had to gain his confidence. But I guess the money helped some too. It should have. It's the greatest little thing there is for winning confidence.

Then finally she came back to me again, came tottering back. She looked all in. You'd almost think that some of the aftereffects had transferred themselves to her, the livid sick color she'd turned. She had the look on her face of someone who has just been granted a quick glimpse down into the bottommost depths of hell from the top of the stairs. And didn't turn away quickly enough.

Her teeth were chattering as she closed the door behind her. "I'd rather be dead," she said. She shuddered and she pulled her shawl around her tight, and the night was hot in Havana. "Boy, could I use a shot of *aguardiente*—after that!" She flung herself down into a chair and held her hair.

"You should have let me go in and tackle it."

She fanned her hand at me without looking around. "You wouldn't have known which end his head was at. And he probably would have pulled a knife on you and run amuck as soon as he got a look at your face. They're apt to be more afraid of a Yank than they are of a Cuban."

I didn't ask her anything; I let her sit for a while and get over it. I kept watching her and thinking, You find gold in the unlikeliest places. Dunghills and ash heaps. She'd done it for me. Gone in there like that for me. Someone she didn't even know back an hour or two. Why? What did she get out of it? What was the percentage? Yes, you find gold kicking around in the funniest places.

She lifted her chin from the back of the chair. "It's Tío Chin, all right," she said quietly. "I can tell by the way he described the layout. He's never seen him himself, this one, but all you have to do is put two and two together. The store is just a front. The place they go for it is a dive called 'Mama Inez.' That's around on the next alley, and it backs up against the store. I know that place; I've passed it often myself. Both under the same roof, get it? There isn't any Mama Inez; that's just the trade name. It's a combination eating place and rumshop; on a close night you can smell it all the way down at the corner."

"Do you think I have any chance of finding out anything if I go in there?"

"No," she said flatly.

"Then what's the—?"

"But you're going over with him. Going through the mill with him. That makes a difference."

"That sounds appetizing. You mean actually buy a pipe and—?"

"Listen, they're not fools in that racket. You think they're wide open to the street, so all you gotta do is hand them a card that says 'Joe sent me?' And then you get a bird's-eye view of the works?"

"All right, I go in and get introduced. They grab me."

"That's what we want, isn't it?"

"It's all right about getting them to grab me. But that's only half of it. How are we going to get the cops in on it? Once I'm grabbed I'm no longer a free agent."

"What do you suppose I'll be doing—sitting up here manicuring my nails? I'll follow the two of you over to this den, *guapo*. At a distance, so he won't notice me. Then after you go in I'll hang around out there in the alley. A girl holding up a doorway is no novelty in this neighborhood."

"How will you know? I won't be able to get word to you. If I signal you before they grab me that'll be too soon. If I wait until after they grab me I won't be able to signal you at all."

"We'll have to work out some sort of a timetable then. Suppose I wait an hour from the time you go in?"

"That ought to be long enough. If they're going to grab me at all they'll have me grabbed by that time. One more thing. How do you know they'll listen to you?"

"The cops? They won't. So I'm not going to waste my time trying to tell them that you're innocent, or that you've been grabbed in there, or anything else. All I'll tell them is that I know where they can find you, that I saw you go in there. They're looking for you already. That'll send them in *prisa* without asking any more questions than that. I'm a stool pigeon, see? I'm trying to pick up a little loose change for myself by handing them this information. Then once they get in, let them find out the rest for themselves.

"It's tricky timing. How'll I know how long an hour is? I don't pack a watch."

"How'll *I* know? I don't either. You can tell how long it is by the way it feels. Didn't you ever try that? It's easy. You can *feel* time just as easy as you can tell it from a clock."

I couldn't help laughing at something that occurred to me just then. "Suppose an hour feels a lot longer to you than it does to me and we miss connections?"

"Ah, cut it out!" she said gruffly. "This is no time to be funny. You may end up laughing on the other side of your face."

There was a soft shuffling sound outside the door.

"Here comes your convoy. He's going to steer you in there and show you the ropes. Otherwise you'd probably never get past the street entrance. You're white, you know, and they don't trust you guys."

I got a little stage fright down under the belt. "Say, I'm not going to have to—try any myself, am I?"

"You better not, *guapo,* if you want to keep our timetable straight. That stuff shoots your sense of time to pieces. It makes a minute seem like an hour, or it can make an hour go by like a minute. I suppose you can fake it in some way if you have to; stick cotton in your nose, or something."

She looked at me half humorously, half sympathetically. "Are you scared?"

"Sure I'm scared," I said irritably. "What do you think I am, anyway—a tin soldier? But I'm going through with it."

"I'm glad you admitted it," she said. "Because if you said you weren't I would have only called you a liar—in my heart. And I don't like to have to do that with my friends. I'm a crook, but I'm an honest crook. I'm scared too—for you. But I'm going through with my part of it." She hitched up her shoulders. "Always remember this. A hundred years from now it'll be all the same to the two of us."

"A hundred minutes from now it'll be all the same to the two of us."

"You better go out there now—before he goes back under standing up and I have to bring him to all over again. I'll step out and make the contact for you."

The last thing she said was, "Don't look around. I'll be behind you on the street."

She opened the door and revealed this flickering, candle-lit picture of horror. You expected it to blow away like smoke, but it stayed there upright.

"Here's my friend, Quon. I told him you'd fix him up. He's been a long time without his sleep."

The cadaver didn't answer, just looked me over. I couldn't tell if he really saw me or not.

To me she said, for stage effect, "Come back and see me when you wake up." And pretended to close the door.

I motioned to him to go down the stairs first, before me. I didn't want to have him falling on top of me when we got halfway down.

He stopped down in the street entrance and took root. Just stood there, as though that was as far as he was going.

I fumbled in my clothes and handed him some money. He fumbled in his and then he got under way again, went out into the alley. So that was the lubrication that had been required.

We shuffled along, down to the mouth of the alley and around it. All of a sudden he spoke to me without turning to look at me. His mouth was sort of half open all the time, anyway, as if he were panting for air; you couldn't tell when he was getting ready to speak and when he wasn't.

"You know La Media Noche long?"

I saw I'd have to watch myself. He wasn't as dopey as he looked.

"From before, when I was in port. I knew her hombre too. I was the friend of both."

It must have been the right answer. I saw him nod shrewdly.

"He lives on in her. She is not for love. The whole street knows that."

We came out of the alley together, turned down the other way, the opposite way from that which I'd taken the time before. Two strange shapes sidling along side by side, bound for a strange place, and with a strange purpose best not inquired into: spread-legged merchant seaman and hunched, bedraggled specter.

There was no light around, and yet he must have been looking at me when I wasn't aware of it. He no longer was, though, when he spoke. That made it all the creepier, as if he had eyes at the side of his head.

"You have never slept before. You haven't any of the marks on you. Our eyes know each other."

My throat tightened up for a minute. "I begin tonight. Life is hard, and I want to forget it for a little while."

He shrugged with the bony epaulets that were his shoulders. "You have paid me."

We went down a new alley, a little wider, a little straighter than the one Midnight lived on. Only a little, though. Ahead, at about the approximate distance that Chin's shop lay from the mouth of the other one, ribbons of light spoked across this one, glimmering through the interstices of an unfurled bamboo blind stretched across an entryway. I knew that must be it, before we'd gotten to it, because of its parallelism to the hidden curio store on the other side. I was scared and started to feel crawly long before there was anything to be scared or feel crawly about.

It was like a last port of call. And the path that had led me to it through the night had been so black and so full of fear, and downgrade all the way, lower and lower, until at last it had arrived at this bottomless, abyss, than which there was nothing lower.

The bars of light made cicatrices across us. He reached in at the side and slanted up one edge of the pliable blind, made a little tent-shaped gap, and bowed his way in through there. His hand, lingering behind a moment, made a hook to me to follow.

For a second I stood alone, livid weals striping me from head to foot. I kneaded my face with one hand in a half circle, starting up at my forehead and ending around past my mouth and chin. Then I hiked up the blind and stooped through in turn.

CHAPTER XI

IT WAS A DIVE the like of which I've never seen before or since. There are wild spots all over the world—the Vieux Port at Marseille, the Casbah at Algiers, the Boca down at Buenos Aires; this was a distillation of them all, stewing in one small suffocating caldron, smelling and sweating and swearing and snarling. Outside, at least, the night had been clear, even in the reeking alley. In there it was like stepping into a lighted fog. A sort of vapor illuminated from below. You could see everything through it, but nothing was clean-cut; it was all hazy and slanted.

Poor Sloppy's, with its harmless raffishness, seemed like the Ritz by comparison. It was crawling with humanity; they made you think of maggots, squirming all over every square inch of space under the flashing, blurred oil lanterns. Black, brown, tan, yellow—every race—and all of them garbage of each particular race. There were whites there too, but they were in a minority to the others: beachcombers, tramp seamen, wharf rats, thugs. The race lines cut across the sexes, but that was only one more horro added to the rest. At least I got no second looks as slouched in after him from the street, cap pulled low.

We wormed our way through to the back, he in the lead stepping between people and over them, and sometimes o them, to get there. A hand reached for my shoulder—woman's, I suppose—but then trailed weakly off it agai as I kept going without looking around.

He sat down on a wooden bench against the back wa

that had a displaced table partially before it, the other end weighted down by someone's inert, sodden head. I spotted a momentarily unclaimed chair and drew it up and sat down to the side of him.

No one paid any attention to us; we were just two more maggots in the squirming mass.

"What happens now?" I said finally.

"Nothing yet. It is too soon. They see you with me."

A waiter in a sweat-mildewed silk shirt brought us two rancid beers that smelled as though the keg they'd come out of had grown moss on the inside. It was the sort of place where you paid for what you got as it was brought up, otherwise it wasn't left on the table. They had to do it that way, with their sort of clientele.

There was an inconspicuous door offside to us, giving through the rear wall. Beside it there was a cashier of sorts, sitting poring over a Chinese newspaper. The waiters would go to him one by one and transfer their takes, when they had accumulated sufficiently to make it worth while.

"Do we have to drink this stuff?" I said finally.

"You smoke cigarette," he said. "I show you."

We both lit up a couple, and I watched to see what he'd do. He didn't seem to do anything, just sat there somnolent, letting it burn away between his fingers. He didn't bother to knock off the end. After a while a cone of ash dropped of its own weight and fell there on the table top.

I looked around at the cashier. He was still engrossed in that up-and-down Chinese newspaper. You could see only the top of his face over it, just the eyes. They didn't seem to see anything but what was printed there below them.

"Do not turn your head so."

I turned back again.

He rested his forearm flat on the table and brushed the ashes off with a swirling motion of his whole sleeve, using his elbow for a pivot. Two swipes one way, then two swipes the other.

The fastidiousness didn't go with his mangy condition, so I figured that must be the password right there. I gave my cigarette a snap to unload it over the table, then I put my own arm down and swung it, twice one way, twice the other.

I looked around. The cashier had left his perch, as though

he'd gotten tired of reading just then. He opened the door, went in, and started to close it after him. His head gave a little quirk, from our direction over to his, just before he did so. Then it closed after him.

Quon's bony fingers landed on my arm, held it down. "Wait, not yet. There are many eyes in this place."

We sat there a minute longer. Then he took the brake off my forearm. "You go first. In through there, where he did. Walk slow. Say nothing. I will follow."

I got up and lingered by the table a minute on my feet. Then I started to drift over that way. You couldn't walk straight in that littered place, anyway; you had to zigzag and detour, so that made it easy to look aimless.

I got over beside the door and glanced casually around. No one seemed to be paying any attention. I pulled it narrowly open and went in and pulled it right after me.

The noise choked off, and I could hear myself think for the first time since I'd come into the place. There was a forlorn, gloomy passageway leading ahead, with a single oil lantern to light it and a ladderlike stair structure rising steeply at right angles to it and disappearing up through a sort of transom or trap.

The cashier was standing there in the gloom, motionless, as though he were waiting for me.

He said, "You wish something?"

I didn't answer.

He said, "You have come in the wrong door. The way out is over on that side."

A shot of noise and fuzzy light came in, and Quon closed the door after him and was standing there.

He moved close to the cashier and seemed to get some ashes on his sleeve. He brushed it off with grave concern, the way he had the table out there before. Twice one way, twice the other.

"My hand is not very steady," he apologized.

"Perhaps you would like to rest," the cashier suggested. But I was the one he was worried about. He kept watching me.

I took the cue and negligently fanned my hand across the guy's sleeve, the same way Quon had. It occurred to me even at the moment that it was a silly sort of mumbo-jumbo, but if that was the routine, that was the routine.

"Perhaps a short nap, a little siesta—" the cashier purred.

"Could stand," I said.

The cashier rubbed his hands together suggestively.

I slipped him one of the bills Midnight had returned to me, then a second one for Quon.

He didn't seem to take them, but they went, were gone. Like doing card tricks. "See upstairs; maybe they will be able to do something for you." He went over to the foot of the stair ladder, called up something in Chinese. A guttural answer came back through the trap opening.

Quon nudged me to go ahead. *"Suba,"* he said. I started to climb up.

I could smell it the minute my head came clear of the floor. It was terrible. But I hadn't expected roses. I tried to breathe as sparingly as possible.

There was something peculiar about the stair flight. It wasn't built in. When I got to the top I saw there was a grappling hook attachment to it; it could be drawn up bodily from above, on the order of a fireman's extension ladder, cutting off the second floor from below. Then there were two winged flaps that could be folded together over the gap in the ceiling, obliterating it. A handy piece of carpentry in case of a raid.

There was a figure standing up there, waiting, as I slowly came up through the floor. Villainous-looking, but then I didn't expect kewpies around this setup. He was holding a lantern out stiff-armed to get a good look at us as we came through. The rest of the place up there was just oblique shadows slanting off from that small core of light in all directions. I stepped clear, and after a moment the ghostly figure of Quon joined me.

We were in a sort of passage, the mate to the one below. One end of it led into a sort of cavernous chasm, with a faint red glow peering from it offside.

He beckoned us after him with curt contempt and went toward there. The lantern, doling out background to us as he went along and then obliterating it again, showed me a fairly broad opening without any door, a slanted chair alongside it where he kept watch. Then on the inside, when we'd followed him through, there was a small charcoal brazier squatting on the floor. That was where the red glow had been coming from. Ranged around it on three sides were bunks in two tiers.

The reek of the gum was overpowering in here. But there wasn't a sound. Not a whisper. You couldn't tell if there was anyone in those bunks or not. Or whether they were out cold, or watching us stealthily, or what. I think that added to the horror, that eerie silence. A grunt or a sigh would have been something, at least.

I was groggy with fright. I knew—or at least I hoped—that I was going to get over it in a little while; you can get used to anything, but it sure was on full right then. I could feel sweat pumping out all over my forehead, and it came out cold and oozy.

He splashed watery lantern light up at a couple of the bunks, decided against them—maybe because there was somebody already in them, although I couldn't see and didn't try to—then shifted to another direction and splashed it up at a couple more. Then he gave us the go-ahead with his thumb and a grunt. He might have been a cutthroat himself, but he hadn't much use for anyone who frequented this place; that stood out all over him.

I bent down and crawled in, with my insides trying to stay behind. It was like—I don't know how to say it—getting into a coffin. No, worse—a coffin's clean, at least; you're the first one that's used it.

Quon put his knee to the wooden sideboard, and I gave him a vicious push back. "Get out of here!" I grated. He came back and did it again. Then I saw that he was trying to climb up to the one above, and I let him alone.

When his form had writhed from view and I could see out again, the attendant was bending toward me, holding a pipe extended. I took it with both hands and held it broadside, as though it were some sort of reed instrument, and he turned and slippered over to the brazier by the door and started to fan it up a little.

I was surprised at how heavy the thing was. I reached down inside the seaman's jumper Midnight had provided me with and got hold of my undershirt and wrenched off a piece of it. I shoved that into my mouth, wadded it up good, and then I let the pipe rest against it. And I still felt like everything was coming up behind it.

He came back holding a pinch of live coal with a pair of hand tongs, and dropped that into the pipe. The pill he placed on a little, flat, buttonlike saucer out near the end of the pipe. It was supposed to sit there and cook.

Then he let me alone, before I keeled over out of sheer repulsion, and turned his attention to the top bunk.

Then he knocked off and went back to his post outside the door. He took the lantern out with him, and that reversed the tone scheme, made it gloomy in here and dimly lit out there. It was like being awake in the middle of a nightmare.

I put the devilish thing down fast the minute he'd gone. I was scared stiff a little of it might get me, anyway, even from that short insulated contact. I hauled the wadding out and spit about sixty-two times, muffling it with the piece of torn shirt.

Then I just stayed there, propped on my elbow, and sweated some more, and finally I started to cool off and the goose-pimples to smooth out on my skin. My teeth wanted to chatter too—I don't know why, this long after—but I curbed them and they got over it.

It *felt* like it was about half an hour now, and even if my sense of time was fast, I figured I'd better get started and see what I could do.

I sat up first and took off my shoes. They were Western shoes, or whatever you want to call them—hard-soled shoes—and I wanted to get up on him quietly. I left them behind on the bunk, swung my feet to the floor, and started to pay out my stocking soles in the direction of the den opening.

He wasn't quite back behind the screening wall. The way he had his chair, I could see a thin slice of him sticking out beyond it: a strip of his head and one shoulder and arm.

I'd come in there with just my bare hands, but I couldn't risk any noisy wrestling matches. I not only wasn't sure I'd come out ahead, but the whole thing had to be swift and soundless, or it was no good to me. I reached down by the brazier and picked up the hand tongs he'd used before. They weren't very large, but they were iron and plenty heavy enough for what I wanted them for. I brought them along with me, poised up high, the last few creeps.

The way he was sitting, I had to take the side of his head. And even to get at that I had to circle out a little, offside to him, which was risky business. The doorframe shielded most of the top and back of it from me. I had a good hunch he was awake, too, although he was sitting there motionless.

The corner of his eye caught my motion at the last minute, but it was already too late. He started to swing his head around to me, and that just gave me what I wanted. I swung just once, like a pile driver—there was no time for second tries in this—and he sucked in his breath, trying to build up to a yell, but it never got up that far. He slid off the chair sideways and sideswiped the wall like a turning wheel and crumpled to the floor. I waited to see if it had taken, and it had taken.

I picked him up from under the arms and hauled him around into the bunkhouse with me and out of sight behind the doorway. If bleary eyes from the bunks saw me doing it, it was just one more unreal scene from their dreams, I suppose. No one stirred; there wasn't a sound. I tied and gagged him up with rags from the bunk I'd been in myself. Then I went out and picked up the lantern and took a good look around to see what I was up against.

There was only one logical direction in which to go from here, and that was along the dimly perceived passage toward the back. To go down the stair ladder again was no good; I'd simply find myself back where I'd started.

I struck out and started cautiously along it in my stocking feet, watering it with the lantern as I went. I passed a couple of doors, but when I nosed into them they seemed to be simply small supply or storage cubicles stacked with empty cartons and packing cases. These looked, by the telescoped way they were piled up, as though they were being reserved for future use instead of being discards that had already been used. For what purpose, I could imagine.

I kept going, and finally the passage dead-ended in a flat surface that at first sight seemed to be simply the same cracked, mildewed plaster that had lined it all along the way. Passages don't end like that for no reason, though, with a lot of vacant space going to waste where they seem to be leading to. And, furthermore, Midnight had said that the Mama Inez premises backed up against the building housing Tío Chin's store.

So I gave it a thump for luck, and it gave out the sound of wood backing. Then I tested the side wall, and that was genuine plaster. I brought the lantern up closer, and I could see what it was. A very clever paint job hiding a door, complete down to cracks and mottled damp patches. It would have fooled anyone, even in better light than I had.

I fingered around it for a while, and finally I located a keyhole bedded invisibly down within one of the blacker cracks, over at the side. Just about where a keyhole should be in a door, but with no knob or anything to give it away.

I turned and retraced my steps all the way back to my original point of departure. I found the clouted bunkhouse attendant still lying quietly where I'd left him. He was bleeding a little out of one ear; hadn't come to yet. I did what I should have done in the first place, fumbled all through his clothing. I turned up, among other things, a long skinny iron key, and that looked like what I was after. I went back with it, aimed it at the crack, and it belonged. The keyhole swallowed it up to the hilt. I could hear a lock flush open, but the door continued to adhere. I pummeled it a little around the edges to spring it, and it broke and slanted outward. I picked up my lantern and took it in with me.

If I hadn't done anything else yet, at least I'd linked up the two separate segments or cells: the dope den and Tío Chin's store. Now all I had to do was link up the killing at one end of them and Ed Roman, in Miami, at the other end of them, and I'd have a straight line running all the way back, without a break, from the killing to Ed Roman in Miami.

But the night was getting old, and my hour was nearly gone.

CHAPTER XII

I DIDN'T GET VERY far. For a minute it looked as if I'd walked into a boxed-up bulkhead or dummy closet of some sort. The lantern light and I snubbed our noses against unbroken wooden surfacing two paces or less in from the door. There was a little amputated alley formed there, wider than it was deep, but not very much of either. Wood-walled at the sides too. I stood there blocked, with the lantern reflection bent upward into a perpendicular sheet in front of my eyes, looking at planed wood grain from an inch away. But there was no point to it: a locked door, the key to which was retained by the den attendant back there, leading into a blind niche like this.

I pressed against the frontal section first, with elbows, knee, and heel of hand, and that was rigid, fixed. Then I tried it over at the right side and that was too. But when I tackled the left, that paid off. It must have been invisibly hinged above someplace; it swung effortlessly, even loosely, out from the bottom up, like a flap, and I ducked down and went through. Then I caught it and let it back easy, so it wouldn't sound off and give me away.

I found first of all that there was light out here, and electric light at that, so I didn't need the lantern. I turned the little wheel around to kill it, and it gave off a whiff of oil stench and croaked. I set it down against the wall.

There was a bulb hanging on a drop cord, and someone had left it on.

I looked over the contraption that had admitted me, first

of all. On the outside, the side on which I now was, it was rigged up to look like one of these enormous wardrobes that they have down there, standing nearly ceiling-high. It even had a fake seam running up the front of it, complete with grips and everything; only when you tried to open it that way, it wouldn't open; it was in one piece. In other words, it was simply a trick entryway or exit, from back there to here and vice versa. I noticed a mate to it across on the other side of the room, identical as to width, varnish, and everything else, and wondered if that were a dummy too.

These were evidently Tío Chin's quarters I was in; a sort of combination office and conference room. It didn't have any of the gingerbread oriental trim of the store below, I noticed. For instance, the electric light, as I have said, instead of those phony paper lanterns with inked ideographs on them. This place looked like it belonged to a hardheaded, practical businessman—and probably a damned unscrupulous and crooked one, at that. I said to myself, I thought that was an act, that jolly-Chinese-gargoyle impersonation. He overdid it.

Cheap secondhand Spanish office furniture pitted with wormholes. There were a roll-top desk, chairs, and a table, and then the two top-heavy clothespresses. The only exotic touch in the whole room was a thick fringe of beaded strings hanging over a doorless opening opposite me that led out—and, I suppose, forward, to where his actual living quarters were.

I tried the top part of the roll-top desk first and didn't have much luck with it. It was securely locked. There was one drawer underneath that wasn't, but he was no fool. There were a number of ledgers in it, but when I hurriedly cracked them one after the other, all the entries were in Chinese characters; I couldn't do anything with them.

I stopped short suddenly, held it, with that funny feeling you have of being looked at when you don't know where it's coming from. You sort of freeze, lock your muscles, the instinct being that further motion will betray you. Although by the time the feeling comes it's already too late; your presence has been betrayed by then.

I let the ledgers down the rest of the way into the drawer and slowly turned my head and looked over my shoulder. No one; there wasn't a sound. But there wasn't any breeze or draft in here either, and there was no reason for that beaded fringe over there to be stirring slightly the way it was. Or at least settling back into immobility after just having been slightly stirred. A moment ago they'd been motionless, and now they'd just gotten through wavering.

I hurried over and listened. I couldn't hear anything, not even the stealthiest withdrawing footfall. I parted them and looked out. I couldn't see anything either, just the darkness of an empty passageway. But I could smell something. A whiff of something—the faintest essence of something sweet—whether from a living flower or from floral extract, I couldn't tell; there wasn't enough of it to go by, and I was no expert, anyway. Well, maybe it had always been out there.

I went back to my job again. A wastebasket had nothing to offer but a two-day-old copy of *Diario de la Marina.* I turned my attention to the second clothespress next. It interested me. For one thing, it was backed against the same wall that held the opening with the bead curtain, so that argued that it wasn't simply a secret exit as mine had been. Where there already was an outlet in full view, why bother to have an elaborate dummy one beside it? And secondly, now that I came over closer to it, I saw that it was not quite as identical as I had at first taken it to be. There was a difference of about a foot in height, in favor of this one. Then when I looked down at the base I saw what made it. This one was raised clear of the floor; it stood on legs. The other was based solidly, as it had to be to keep its real purpose secret.

It was rickety as a result of being elevated like that; the whole thing wobbled slightly when I tugged vainly at the grips on the huge doors. One of the legs was shorter than the rest, I saw, and half eaten away with wormholes. The center seam was actual in this case, but it was securely locked. I desisted, afraid of bringing the whole thing down on top of me if I struggled at it any more.

I took a step back from it, and then again I froze as I had the time before. But this time when I turned there was no optical illusion about the beaded fringe suddenly falling still or lightly wavering with aftermath of motion. It was openly, unabashedly tucked back into a small diamond-shaped opening, as if parted by two fingers, and in the center of this an eye was looking through at me. An eye with gummed lashes sticking out like rays all around it. It didn't try to hide itself from me; instead, the split in the fringe widened, ran all the way down to the floor; the whole face came slowly through into the room, and with it the body underneath.

She was the prettiest Chinese girl I'd ever seen, and when they are pretty they shoot the works. She was like a doll and built to the specifications of one. About four-ten or five feet at the most, slim to match, tiny red dot for a mouth that you wondered show she could get food into at all. Her skin was the color of creamy porcelain, the eyes oblique, but just enough to be piquant. She had on apple-green trousers and a turquoise-blue coat, both sprinkled with small white chrysanthemums. She had two coral-pink geraniums packed in her hair just over one ear. She brought back some of that scent I'd noticed in the passage before.

I just stood there with my trap open. And I bet I wasn't the first.

She came in a few steps toward me and then stopped. She dipped her knees demurely.

I put my hand up to the peak of my cap, dropped it again, in answer. It seemed to me to be a supremely silly thing to do, even at the moment I was doing it, but I wasn't quite sure why. I suppose because I had no right to be found there where I was.

But for her part she showed neither surprise nor alarm, I noticed. It was almost as though she'd been expecting my arrival, and been coached to greet me when I came. Her very next words showed that.

"Buenas noches," she said in a flutelike little voice that carried its own musical accompaniment.

I didn't get the whole thing, but I mumbled back at her in kind.

She switched to English; they all seemed to speak it down here.

"Are you the caller my estimable uncle told me he was awaiting here tonight?"

So she was Chin's niece; well, that was the first thing about him I found halfway passable.

I certainly wasn't the caller he was expecting, but I nodded. What else was there to do?

She wanted to make quite sure. "You are Captain Paulsen?" I saw her eyes light briefly on the cap and dungarees. They were what had done it, they'd fooled her. He must be expecting some sea captain up here tonight. And what more likely than it was the one who did the running for them between here and the Everglades coast? The skipper of the launch or cutter the stuff was carried in?

This was starting to sound good. I liked it. I wondered if I could work it to get her to show me around a little by playing on the mistake in identity.

I touched my cap again to confirm her in the erroneous impression.

"He will be here soon. He was unavoidably called out on business."

He should take his time, I thought. This was getting better and better by the minute.

"He asked me to tell you to please make yourself at home while you are waiting."

I will, I promised her, unheard; just leave it to me.

"You came in that way, Captain?" She motioned to the spiked wardrobe.

"Yes."

"It puzzled me how you got here; I wondered why they did not tell me they had admitted you at our other door."

She seemed to take the secret passageway in her stride, I noticed. It didn't match up with that pretty baby face of hers. I wondered just how much she knew about what it was like over there on the other side of the wall. But the more she knew, the more there was for me to find out from her, so why should I give a hoot?

"Your men are down there below?"

She meant in that Mama Inez dive. So evidently the real Paulsen brought some of his hands with him each time he came here. He needed them to cart the stuff to the place where they took it aboard. "Yeah, they're down there," I said.

I didn't want to hurry things up, God knows, but I wanted to sound plausible. And also find out how much time I could count on for myself. "How soon will your uncle be back, do you think?"

"Soon. He went to see about getting an extra truck. He said one more would be needed tonight. He asked me to tell you this; he said you would understand."

I did: an extra-heavy shipment tonight. Maybe they were having to cut down the number of runs back and forth they were making, so they were trying to make up for it by doubling on the amount they carried each time.

"Can I get you some tea, Captain, while you are waiting?"

That was about the one thing I could have done without beautifully right then: sitting drinking tea at a time like that!

I shook my head.

She suddenly corrected herself. She'd obviously never met the genuine captain face to face, but she must have been present behind the scenes at the times of his former visits. She wrinkled up her nose at me. The tiny thing could even be mischievous. "I mean, of course, the kind of tea the captain drinks. The rice wine of my uncle."

I tried to shake my head to that, too, even at the risk of stepping out of character. I wanted to keep her in here with me, where I could get some information out of her.

But before I could stop her she'd dipped her knees again and turned to go back. She brushed open the fringes to go through, and then as she did so something seemed to go wrong. I saw two or three of the strands pull taut after her, and then she stopped and started wrangling with her wrist. A couple of the tricky things must have snarled on some button or ornament she wore on her sleeve.

She tried to free herself, failed, finally threw me an appealing look.

It was my time she was using up, so I was only too glad to hurry over to her, see what I could do.

I groped clumsily through the slanting lines of the things that blurred my sight like rain. She was on one side of them, I on the other.

"Here, at my wrist," she said. "Take hold and see if you can—"

Our four hands met in a sort of bowknot, with the things all messed around them. Instead of making it better, I seemed to be making it worse. Something stung the back of my hand unexpectedly, seemed to hang on for a minute, like when you get a splinter in you, then slid out again. I couldn't see what it was; there were three other hands and all those beaded drippings in the way, and all of them moving around in one place.

I pulled the one it had happened to out of the beaded tangle, blew on it. There was a tiny blue dot there, too small for blood to come through. "What was that?"

"I am so sorry," she purred contritely. "A pin on my sleeve must have scratched you."

But she was free again, I noticed, as mysteriously as she had become snagged. She dipped her knees to me once more, hurried off into the gloom with little midget steps.

I stood there a minute, idiotically looking at the back of my hand, then in the direction in which she'd vanished. Like the chump I was. Then I turned and went back to my futile tinkering with the roll-top desk.

I noticed a change coming over my efforts presently. There was something easier, less strenuous about them. First I thought that it was the roll-top that was resisting less. But it was still down fast, hadn't gone up, so then I could see that it wasn't that. It was my own arms that were using less energy, going at it easier, tricking me into thinking I was having less trouble with the job. I started to feel lazy. What am I doing this for; what's the use? Before I knew it I'd come to a full stop; I was just standing there with my hands on it, but not doing a thing any more.

A little leftover spurt of energy came trickling out after the main reserve had been siphoned off, like a chaser, and I gave one last tug. Like a muscular hiccup. Then it evaporated and I quit and just stood there, inert.

I was starting to feel dizzy. I swayed a little, and instead of trying to open the desk now, I was just using it to help me stand up. It wasn't very steady any more; it kept going over one way, and I'd go over the other; then it would come back my way, and I'd go over the other. We couldn't get together.

I nearly lost my balance altogether, but I managed to hang onto it a moment longer by giving the desk a tight hug from a sprawling position over its top.

The beads split open with a catlike ejaculation, and four men came into the room, one behind the other.

So here they were, and here I was, and time was up.

The fat Tío Chin was foremost. Behind him there was a hard-bitten, skull-faced, birch-blond individual, about six feet tall, wearing a peaked cap somewhat similar to mine and a skimpy pea jacket that looked like it had shrunk in the rain: this time the real launch captain. He looked like a Scandinavian who has been buried three days and dug up again after decomposition has already set in. Behind these two there were a couple of anonymous plug-uglies: I suppose the hands they used to load and unload the stuff. They were whites, but under deep burns that made their faces look as though they'd been smoked and shriveled for a long time by equatorial head-hunters.

But the big change was in Chin himself. This was behind the scenes now, and the feeble-minded celestial act had been discarded, just as I'd suspected when I first saw the room itself. He wasn't wearing his hands plaited together, and when he opened his mouth it was to shoot out better English than I used. The pigtail mustache had vanished, and so had most of the sleepiness and all of the benevolence. The only thing he still had the same was the fat stomach.

They ranged themselves around me, robot-like, matter-of-fact, deadly in their sluggishness. No dramatics, no violence; just sort of an amused superiority that even extended to the two stevedores. They weren't going to be tough; they were going to be playful. They were going to have some sport with me. Cat-and-mouse stuff. With the mouse already very groggy and almost down for the count.

I blinked, and there were eight instead of four of them. Then I blinked again, and they condensed back to four again.

Tío Chin said, "Well! Well, well, well! A customer. What do you think of that, boys? A customer. And after closing hours, too!"

The aluminum-complexioned sea captain furled his lips back to show two white teeth and three black ones. Ten years before, when he did that, it had probably turned out to be a smile; it didn't now any more. "And no von to vait on him, either. You should give better service than this, Chin. You lose money this vay."

Chin said, "Well, we'll take care of that right now." He

bowed in his best store-front manner. "Were you looking for something?" He rapped his palms. "A chair for the customer. Where are your manners?"

A chair seat bit suddenly into the rear hollows of my legs, and I folded down onto it. I sat there looking up at them dully. My eyelids felt like they were putting on weight, kept trying to close. I didn't feel much like repartee. "All right," I said. "All right. You've got me."

The two seamen had lounged back against the wall, grinning, to watch their bosses. The captain sat down on one of the other chairs, facing me. He was too big to sit down like most people, just straight up and down; he took up some of the slack by folding one leg flat across the knee of the other. He was still trying to be coy, and with the kind of face he had, it was ghastly. I guess he didn't get much relaxation; he seemed to be enjoying this. "Maybe he came here looking for somevon," he chuckled. "Vy don't you ask him who he's looking for? I know who he's looking for, I bat you. Show him. Go ahead, show him."

Chin snickered. "Our policy is always to accommodate the customer. Never let him walk out dissatisfied."

"Never let him walk out at all be batter." The launch captain couldn't even laugh right any more; it came out in sputters and burbles, like a leaky steam joint. I expected to see the front of his face blow off. It would have improved his looks, anyway. "Go ahead, show him vat he came to see," he urged. "Don't keep him vaiting."

"You make me give away all my trade secrets, Paulsen." Chin took out a key, opened the front of the clothespress. He pulled the two halves out and stood aside to give me a good look.

The hanging figure looked vaguely familiar, but I wouldn't have been able to identify him for sure, the stat they had him in now. "Peek-ture, for the señor and lady t show their friends?" came back to me. But it was jus association of ideas more than anything else; you couldn' tell who this was any more. He was all crisscrossed wit rope, and they had him dangling by a sort of halte arrangement from under the arms to a hook on a stou rod that ran across the top of the clothespress.

He wasn't dead yet; I could see his chest rising an

falling even from where I was. He was either unconscious or else stunned with abuse. There were purplish discolorations under each eye, and his whole face was lumpy, as if he had the mumps, and his lips were split. I wondered for a minute how it was he hadn't suffocated inside that thing, but then when I looked up I saw that the top was off; there was a wire mesh roofing it instead.

"Is that who you were looking for?" Chin chuckled.

"No," I glowered. "I came here looking for the rat who stuck a knife through my—my—" I couldn't finish it.

Chin closed the wardrobe slabs, gestured emptily. "No sale."

Paulsen smote his knee. "Oh, *now* I know! Vy didn't you say so sooner? Look, I show you a picture of him. How you like to see a picture of him?"

My eyes swerved back to him fast, dulled as they were. He was fumbling inside his jacket. He took out a greasy wallet. Out of that he took a glossy black photographic negative.

"It's not a very good picture I show you," he apologized.

He held it out toward me. I reached for it, and it was a little farther away than it had been. I reached for it again, and again it was just a little too far out of reach.

"Here, take it. I thought you vanted it," he said. That was his idea of being funny. "First you vant it, then ven I give it to you, you don't take it."

I grabbed harder than before, and this time I went over flat on my face on the floor.

I could hear the thunder of their laughter up over my head. My eyes started to droop closed. I didn't care; let 'em laugh.

They weren't through, though. They hadn't had enough. They picked me up again and sat me back on the chair, and with the reverse of equilibrium my eyelids went up again.

Paulsen was holding the negative up toward the light now, squinting at it fondly. "I tell vat's on it," he said. "You can't see gude from vere you are. Is on it the lady's face and yures. Is on it the lady's—" He passed a hand down his own side.

Chin gave him the gutter word for it.

"Is on it the knife, all the way in. Is on it the hand of falla who holds knife. You can't see his face. But on back of hand is small star with five points."

Then he showed me his own, with the deeply inked original tattooed on it. "Yust like this."

"You were the guy," I told him, low. "You were the one did it. There was a cap like yours somewhere near us in the crowd; I can remember that now, but I didn't before—"

He turned languidly to Chin. "You think I should keep this picture? My girl back in the States, maybe she don't like it; it show me with other voman."

Chin was simmering with amusement. "You're prettier than the picture makes you look, Paulsen."

Paulsen nodded. "Maybe I gat another taken sometime." A match flared in his hand, and he brought the two slowly together, the film and the flame, watching me over the top of them to see if I was getting the full effect.

I was. I packed a fist and tried to launch myself at him. He was agile for a guy that tall. He hopscotched his chair back without getting up from it and still holding the flame and negative. I floundered short and would have gone down on my kisser again, but this time the two crewmen caught me around the waist and held me up off the floor. They slopped me back again like dirty water across a deck.

"Now vatch close," Paulsen grinned.

The flame and the negative came together. The film hesitated for a minute, then it started to pick up speed. It burned fast and smokelessly and with a very bright, concentrated flame, the way that stuff does. Then it died down and he was holding nothing between his fingers but just a little smudge.

I felt swell. My head looped down over my wishbone.

Chin's voice was gurgitating with laughter. "Look at him, he's all tired out. Maybe the climate down here doesn't agree with him."

One of the huskies standing behind my chair took a corkscrew twist in my hair, hauled my head up and around again. The pain made my eyes flicker open.

"He needs a change," Paulsen said. "Maybe a little sea air vill brace him up. Nothing better than that. I take him vith me ven I go back tonight, him and that other falla in closet. I take them both vith me. They both very sick men."

"For free?" Chin asked, ingenuous to the gills.

"For free. Part of the vay, anyway."

That "part of the vay" roused me for a minute.

"Are you a good svimmer?" he asked me. "I bat you are not so good as some of the sharks they got between here and the Keys."

Chin grimaced appreciatively. "He hasn't got as good teeth as they have, either."

My head did a side roll, then came back again.

Paulsen clucked concernedly. "He's too tired even to listen to us. He don't hear a vord ve say. Chin, that niece of yours should be ashamed of herself."

Suddenly the tempo of their slow, sadistic baiting had busted wide open; a quick, hustling activity had taken its place almost before I knew it. My senses were too torpid to be able to keep up very well. The hinged flap at the side of the dummy wardrobe I'd come through myself earlier suddenly flew up without warning, and I got a blurred glimpse of a figure standing there, half in, half out, jabbering something in firecracker Chinese to Chin, then whisking back out of sight again.

Chin got a move on, caught up in the new pace. "Tie this guy up," he flung at the two huskies. He could move quickly when he had to, in spite of that big bay window he carried. He sprinted out through the bead drops, called something in Chinese. A girl's voice answered from up front somewhere. Then he came back again, ran through to the dummy wardrobe, and went in behind it. It was wide enough to admit him, though I hadn't thought it would be.

He called some orders through at that end—quite a few of them—and I could hear pulleys squeaking and woodwork thudding, as though they were raising that detachable stair out there and obliterating the trap.

Meanwhile the two seamen had me helpless between them, were lashing my arms together behind my back with a length of rope.

Chin reappeared again, puffing now from his own quickness but with a complacent look, as though everything had been taken care of.

"Vat happened? Vat's the row?" Paulsen asked him.

"We've got company. We're having a little visit from the police downstairs." Then at the nervous start the captain made: "Just sit tight. Don't try to leave now. You're all right while you stay up here. It's nothing; we've had them before. It'll be over in a minute or two. They simply go straight through from the back of the drink shop and keep going until they find themselves out in the open again, in the alley on the other side, like a puppy chasing its tail. They wouldn't come up here in a million years. They never have yet."

"I don't like it, having 'em right under my feet like that," Paulsen said skittishly and shifted a little, as though the floor were hot.

"There is nothing to attract their attention to us. People don't look *up* at a ceiling when they come into a place; not even police on a raid. Not unless there is a stair line to draw their gaze up after it. Otherwise their eyes follow the lines that are already there; in this case, straight ahead. It's very simple and very surefire."

The hour. The hour must be up.

Chin motioned lazily toward the wardrobe. "Put him in there with the other one until they've gone. Then you can take them both with you in the truck, along with the other bales. We'll fix up a couple of sacks."

He came over close and peered into my face. "He's still awake, but you can hardly tell it." He smirked. "Just one little spark left. Watch it go out." He rounded his cheeks and blew a puff of breath at me.

Then his face sort of slipped backward. I didn't know if he was moving or I was. "What kick has he?" I heard him say from far away. "After all, it's an easy way to die."

I could still hear and feel longer than I could see. I could feel them pick me up and carry me between them, hoist me up into the big cavelike thing. Then I could feel a sort of halter they must have made between my arms in back catch onto something, and I swung there loose, stocking feet clear of the clothespress bottom.

Then it got dark, or rather the lingering red on the lining of my eyelids, which were down already, dimmed to purple and then to black. Wood closed against wood, and a key turned and withdrew.

Everything got blurred and comfortable. There was no

more trouble in the world; there was no more murdered love; no more cops. No one you had to be afraid of, no one you tried to get, and no one who tried to get you. Twilight of the mind, with night coming on fast. Not the night of the calendar; the night of the being.

Even the unnatural rearward hoist of my arms stopped hurting. But I was straight up and down, and I wanted to sleep the way you were supposed to sleep, the long way. I tried to lie down a couple of time and I couldn't; my feet just skidded.

Over the open top of the thing the sound of a voice, dim, unrecognizable, coming from far away, roused me flickeringly and for the last time. A snatch of something being said out there: "They're going already. . . . They'll be out in a minute. . . . I told you . . . I don't know—some street girl around here who was probably thrown out of the drink shop and wanted to get even. . . . They're going to arrest her for giving a false alarm. . . ."

I didn't know who it was who was going, and I didn't care; good, let them go. All I wanted to do was sleep. But I wanted to sleep lying down, the way I was used to; it felt tight this way.

I tried again and leaned forward. Somebody, something, wouldn't let go of me. I leaned forward with all my might, tried to throw myself down.

My head came to rest against the locked front of the clothespress. I don't know how much a head weighs. Mine felt like it weighed a ton. But even a little added weight is sometimes enough to tip a scale. . . .

I was *falling* asleep. *Falling*—I could feel myself going down into it headfirst. Sleep sure was deep, for you to fall into it like that. Somebody in my dreams screamed, "Look out! It's coming down—"

The last flicker of consciousness went with a sort of soft thud that might have made a big thundering noise all around me, that might have even shaken the whole building, but that I didn't even hear or feel inside me, where I now was.

I was lying flat now, the way you should sleep.

I didn't know if this was sleep or death. But even if it was death, gee, it sure felt good to die.

CHAPTER XIII

I CAME TO AGAIN—you always do, until the last time, and the last time is the time that counts—and I couldn't get where it was I was supposed to be at first. All I could tell was it was day again; there was light coming in a barred window opposite me, and the night, that long Havana night, was over at last. The night that had seemed to last forever while it was going on. When it had begun we'd been taking in the town in an open carriage together, I remembered, about to start a new life. And look at me now.

I was on some sort of cot. I still had on my waterfront duds, or at least part of them, but somebody had thrown a threadbare blanket carelessly over my legs and left my feet sticking out at the other end. I pushed myself up on my arm, and for a minute everything went wavy, then settled down again.

I looked around. There was that window with the bars on it, but that doesn't mean anything down there; they all have them below the second story—custom of the country. Otherwise you couldn't tell what the place was. It wasn't an out-and-out cell; just a shade or two above that—sort of detention room, I guess. There was a calendar put out by a Cuban brewery tacked up on the wall, but they'd quit peeling the leaves off at February. February 1934, I might add.

There was a door, and just as my eyes got to it, it opened and a cop looked in at me. Just on a knob turn; no business about locks and keys or anything. *"Está despierto, Inspector,"* I heard him call out to someone. He pulled his head back again and closed it before I could say anything, but he was a cop; I was pretty sure of that.

Well, the other bunch didn't have me, but they did. Back where I'd started again.

There was a stage wait of several minutes, then it reopened, and the same cop held it back for someone else to come through. Acosta showed up holding a batch of papers in his hand. He stopped short to say something over his shoulder by way of postscript to them in the other room, and I caught a glimpse through the doorway of a starchless figure being hauled off between two cops, legs dragging across the floor behind him, a peaked cap on the back of his head. Then the door was closed.

Acosta spanked the sheaf of papers he was holding. "¡Por fin!" he said jubilantly.

I didn't know if he meant me or the papers.

"Well, how's the ex-suspect?" he grinned.

I blinked at him, logy. Brilliant repartee.

"Ex. You know, used to be?"

"You mean I'm in the clear?"

He chuckled. "Well, *carajo,* where you been all night?" he jeered good-naturedly.

I answered that with a slight but expressive moan.

"I know," he answered for me. "In an overturned wardrobe closet, flat on your face, among other places. We pulled you out headfirst through the top of it, easier than standing it up again; it would have taken a hydraulic jack."

The cop came in with black coffee, and I got most of it down my chin, but enough went in to do me some good. It's wonderful stuff for a hang-over from a hypodermic. Then they gave me a cigarette, and it went up and down in my hand like a yo-yo.

Acosta was beaming as if he loved everybody in the world—well, everybody on his side of the fence. I guess cops do when they've just cleaned up a case.

"Boy, you talk about near misses!" he jabbered. "My raiding party was already outside in the alley again after going straight through to the store side and coming back to report nothing suspicious. If they'd let well enough alone, we'd have been already on our way. But, like fools, they called me back inside again for a minute—I suppose to give me a little additional soft soap. While I'm standing there in the passage talking it over, *boom!* I thought the whole building was coming down on my head. A little stream of plaster comes spilling down from the ceiling, right on both my shoulders. I blew my whistle, and we closed in again, and this time we went *upstairs* as well as down."

He quirked his head. "It was worth the trip, believe me. We found a den going full blast—we suspected there was one somewhere around here, but we'd never been able to locate it until now. And we found enough raw opium, packed up and ready to go out, to choke an ox. And, lastly, we found you and your wardrobe companion. There was quite a time up there. They lost their heads, made the mistake of pulling guns on us, so we—how you say it—went to town on them."

"Who'd you get?"

"We got 'em all. But some of them not in serviceable condition any more. We came in from both sides, see, and nailed them in the middle. They didn't have anywhere to go."

"They've got someplace to go now," I growled resentfully.

"Don't worry, their tickets are bought and they're on the train."

"There was a picture that would have saved me. If I only could have got hold of it when I tried—"

"Oh, we've got that ourselves," he assured me. "It's Exhibit A."

"I saw him burn it in front of my very eyes!"

"That was the negative. Campos made one print of the picture before they broke in on him at his place. He put it where he always puts his prints to dry out, and so they won't curl up at the edges. Under the mattress of his cot. Not a very professional system, but then he works on a shoestring, anyway. So they took the negative, but they missed that. He'd already seen what was on it, and he told us where to look for it as soon as he came back to consciousness."

"How is he; did he pull through?" I asked eagerly.

"He's in the hospital. They gave him a pretty bad shellacking, but he'll probably be up and around again in plenty of time for us to use him as a material witness when your friend in there goes on trial for murder. Between the attack on him and the attack on you and the picture and Paulsen's own confession, which is what I'm holding in my hand, I don't think we've got much to worry about."

"Paulsen? He broke?"

"Into crumbs." He laughed. "We just laid down the rolling pins a little while ago, before you woke up."

He flipped over a couple of the closely typed papers. "He's been giving dictation all morning. Third draft, no errors. We've got it down to the last comma. . . . The minute you two stepped out of the store—he was back; Chin had him waiting back there—he called him to the entrance and pointed you out to him."

"Didn't care who it was, did he? Had never even seen us before."

"What was it to him? Just a little job on the side. Chin showed him the knife. 'This is the one he thinks he just bought. He's carrying the receipt for it in his pocket right now. I switched them on him when I was wrapping them up.' Then, he says, Chin said to him, 'You follow him and switch them back again—this time *through the woman's skin*. Be sure you get the other one away from him.' Then he gave him some of the same green paper and rubber bands as he'd wrapped around the original knife."

"So he didn't actually take it from my pocket and strip it then and there in the crowd."

"Of course not, how could he? That was to make your defense sound fishy to us."

"Which it sure did."

"He got your own away from you before you even got anywhere near the bar. He saw that you were going in there, and he got in ahead of you. You squeezed right past him when you were wriggling your way through the crowd, pulling her after you. You even helped him without knowing it; to make it easier, you had your coat unbuttoned. The pressure of his body against yours in that thick crowd peeled it back, and the knife was too long for the pocket anyway. It practically came out in his hand.

Then he worked his way over after you, as soon as you had found a place to stand, knifed her with the one Chin had given him, threw the decoy paper and the rubber bands on the floor, so they'd be found lying there as if they'd come out of your own pocket."

"Thought of everything, didn't they?"

"But the photographer got his hand."

"So now you've got *him*. And he got his orders from Chin."

"He got his orders from Chin," he agreed. "He admits that."

"So far so good. Now what about getting it out of Chin where *he* got *his* orders from?"

"It stops there."

I sat up straighter on the cot, parking the coffee mug with a clunk. "What d'you mean, it stops there? You're going to punish the hand and let the brain go?"

He made passes with his hands. "We can't hook up the two together. We can't prove which brain the hand was working for."

"Look," I said, "give it to me straight. Never mind the parabolas or parables or whatever you call them."

"Tío Chin is dead," he said. "He died a couple hours ago, after being unconscious ever since the raid."

"What the hell's the matter with those men of yours?" I flared. "Why'd they have to be so hot-triggered? He was fat; he couldn't have put up much of a fight! Why didn't they try to take him al—?"

"My men didn't do it. He didn't put up any fight at all. He just sat there quietly waiting, when he saw that he was trapped and couldn't get out. We broke in the room where he was, and we found him sitting there in a Chinese robe, drinking a cup of tea, his niece bowing her head against his knee. I thought I saw him making a face, as if it was bitter, but we didn't catch on in time; there was too much excitement going on. We were on the lookout for gunplay, not tea drinking. The girl died first, and he passed out a few minutes after we got him down here. It must have been a triple overdose. Even the stomach pumps couldn't bring him back."

That was one guy I never thought I'd be sorry to hear was dead, but I was; I sure was. I wanted him back as badly as if I'd liked him, instead of hating his guts the way I had. "Where does it stand now? Where does that leave it?"

"The connecting link is broken," Acosta told me. "We have the man who did the actual knifing, and he will be tried for murder. But we can't go back any farther than that. There is a gap now. The middleman is gone. It was a relay, from one to the next."

"But it was Roman!" I socked myself hotly on the chest. "*I* know that! I'm as sure of it as I'm sitting here! You ought to too. Anybody— The order originated with him. He was the starting point."

"That's just an opinion, not a fact. And I agree with it myself as an opinion. But I can't issue an extradition warrant on the strength of an opinion. I have to have proof before I can proceed against anyone, not an opinion. Not even when it's my own opinion."

I crouched over low and took a close look at the floor, as if I was trying to make out something written on it. And in invisible ink at that. "But Chin never set eyes on either one of us in his life before until last night, maybe half an hour before it happened. What reason? Doesn't your own common sense tell you—?"

"That's probably true. Although you can no longer prove even that, because Chin is dead now. But it also works in reverse. Paulsen has never set eyes on Roman in his life either; doesn't even know there is such a person. And we know that's true because he gave us everything else; why wouldn't he have given us that? He would have been only too glad to pass the buck if he could have. He can't."

"He's been running the stuff up there. He must have turned it over to someone. He didn't just dump it on the beach."

"A man with a truck picked it up each time, a man that initialed a receipt and didn't give him any name. And that man certainly wasn't Roman. The initial was just a code okay. Chin knew what it was; Paulsen didn't have to. Paulsen was working for Chin, out of this end. Not for anyone at all out of the other end. And even if *that* trail could be traced back eventually to Roman, yours is a different trail, and yours can't. He gave the order for that killing to one man and one alone, and that man is dead now, without having spoken. Don't you see? It's gone forever."

"And even if you had Roman right here is your jurisdiction, in custody here in Havana, you couldn't bring him to book for murder, couldn't proceed against him?"

"No," he said. "What evidence is there against him?"

I stood up slowly, as if I'd lost all further interest in the conversation. Well, to tell the truth, I had. "That seems too bad," was all I said thoughtfully. "It seems too bad."

I shoved my hands in my pockets and looked at him suddenly. "What's my own status? Am I being held here as a witness, or what?"

I noticed he took a minute or two to answer. "By rights, you should be," he said to me in a hesitant sort of way. "It's a murder trial, after all, and your presence will be necessary as a witness." Then he passed a hand over his chin. "But let's stretch a point and say you're free under your own cognizance."

"I'll be in Havana when the trial opens," I assured him grimly.

He watched me drift over toward the door and put my hand on it.

"Where are you going?"

"There's an old saying in my language. To change it around a little, I'm going to see a dog—about a lady."

CHAPTER XIV

THERE I WAS, WALKING back along the same way again, the way out to Hermosa Drive, just like the day I'd found the wallet and first got the job. Only now I knew what was up ahead; then I hadn't. Now I was walking toward death; then I'd been walking toward love. It was night now, to match the difference of my aim; then it had been light.

I didn't mind the walk. I didn't mind the time it took. I wanted it to be late when I got there. Good and late. That's why I didn't try to hitch my way out, as I easily could have done. I wasn't in any hurry. I was sure of getting there. Nothing could have stopped me.

I plodded along under the stars, unhurried, even-paced, steady, and sometimes a breeze from the sea would cut across me and play around with me a little and then go on its way again. Then the night would be calm and still again, like it had been before. Once in a while a car would streak by, making a comet path out of its heads that slowly dissolved again after it was well gone.

It's a funny feeling, to keep going and know that ahead of you, when you get where you're going, two men are going to die. Or at least you'd think it would be, but it wasn't. I didn't feel anything at all about it. I didn't even ate much any more. I was like all frozen up about it. I suppose that's a bad way to feel, but it makes it awfully easy to do a thing like that. You're just a machine, and the switch handle has been thrown away; you can't be turned off any more.

Those stars looked funny, winking to each other, giving each other the eye, all over the vault above me, as if they knew what was up and had seen so much of this, it was an old story to them. As if they were saying, "There is goes again."

It must have been about three, I guess, when I got out to Hermosa Drive; I don't know for sure. I turned off the main highway and walked down to the place. They had the gate locked now, cutting across the right of way, but that didn't stop me. I knew by heart the places where the wall was easiest to get over. I walked along it till I found one of them, all the way down toward the shore, where it ran down into the sand. When the tide was low, like it was now, all you had to do was reach and pull yourself up over it from standing level. But even if the tide had been high, I think I would have swum out and around the end of it and come floating back on the inside. He even had the ocean staked off in front of his place; it was his own private property.

That's one thing those who live in fear should learn: you can keep a man out, but you can't keep death out.

I was squirming up the beach now, coming at the place from the front. It was built to face the ocean, as I've told you. That door at which I'd always picked them up with the car was in reality the rear door, though it was the only one they ever used.

I was on the inside now. They'd already stopped living but they didn't know about it yet.

The little private *cabañas* that they'd used for sun-bathing stood up there over to one side, black against the white gleam of the sand. They looked like sentry boxes. There was a low, rumbling sound, and something came rushing at me from around in back of them, too quick to be focused.

They had a dog on the inside, Job's dog. They thought that was protection enough; that and the gate and the wall. It would have been ordinarily. He would have torn to pieces anything on two legs he found on the wrong side of the fence.

I stopped short and held it, to see if I was going to take or not. He curbed his onslaught only at the last minute and sent up a spray of sand all over my legs, trying to dig in. When you've once made friends with a dog it doesn't wear off again. That's the difference between a dog and men.

"Hello, Wolf," I said, "I'm back," and groped for his skull a couple of times.

He was more of a nuisance trying to love me up than he had been trying to chew me up. He kept getting in my way.

"All right, go back to slep," I said; "this has nothing to do with you."

The lights were all out in the house. I'd never had a key to the house, so I'd have to go in there and get them the best I could. I didn't want to ring and mix Job up in it. Job was all right; I had nothing against him. I'd sat and eaten my meals at the same table with him the whole time I was there.

I walked around to the side and followed that back, to where Roman's windows were. That terrace he had outside his room helped a lot; that made a break, a notch in the straight up and down of the walls. I used the window indentations below for footrests—they had these Spanish-type iron grilles over them—and managed to get a grip on them, then hoisted myself up and over.

Then I stood a minute and looked down. Wolf was sitting there on his haunches and watching, head cocked to one side in curiosity. I thumbed him back toward the beach, but he didn't move.

I turned to face the way I was going. He had the windows all open; you just stepped in, without even lifting your feet. The room was dark and quiet, but I knew he was in it. I could hear him breathing and I could smell the alcohol he'd brought back on his breath from wherever it was he'd been earlier tonight.

I felt my way in and around and over the way in which I remembered the bed to have been, that one and only time I was ever up here before, that first day.

I traced the bottom of it with my hand and felt along the side of it, and when I'd gone far enough up toward the head, I sat down on the edge of it, close beside him. The mattress sank a little under my weight, but he didn't seem to feel it.

I wanted him to see me. I wanted him to know whom he

was getting it from when he got it. I reached out for a little lamp he had there close beside the bed and clicked it on. Twin halos of light sprang out, one at each end of the shade, and showed up our faces and a little of the margin around them. The shade itself was opaque, to rest the eyes.

Then I just sat back and waited for the shine to percolate through to him, sitting on the bias to him. It took some time. He was sleeping like a log. He didn't miss her. Murder agreed with him. He must have been brought up on it. He must have been weaned on it. Good; I was going to see that he got some more.

I let him take his own time about waking up. I sat and waited quietly on the edge of the bed, right next to him, looking at him, watching his face. I thought of all the ugly people I'd run into in Havana the night before, and there'd been some beauts. Quon the dope fiend, and that Danish sea captain. But he was the ugliest of the lot, this man here. To me he was, anyway. Because he'd killed the thing I loved.

The light started to filter through to his brain. He got restless. He tried to turn over away from it and get it off his face. I took him by the shoulder and eased him back again the way he'd been the first time. But not violently, just by a sort of indirect pressure.

The lids of his eyes flickered, made a couple of false starts to go up. Then suddenly they made it all the way, stayed that way, and the thing was under way at last.

First there was just disbelief in them; he thought he was having a bad dream or the light was playing tricks on him. He shuttered them rapidly two or three times in succession to get me out of them. I stayed in, and he had to believe it.

I watched the fear come into them slowly, changing them, making them glassy and swelling them.

"Hello, Roman," I said. "Nice night for dying, isn't it?"

His voice was still asleep. He had to shake it to wake it up. "Jordan," he whispered hoarsely. "Jordan."

I put my open hand to the base of his throat and just left it there, resting lightly, relaxedly. "Don't try to call for him in full voice," I said. "Because I can stop it, down here, quicker than you can get it all the way up and out. You'll only bring the thing on all the quicker. While you're quiet, you're alive."

The collar of his pajamas was in the way a little, so I took my other hand and spread the wings farther out, first one and then the other, where they wouldn't interfere. He still went in for those candy-striped satins, I saw; this time black and gold.

He kept his voice down to a sandpapered whisper. Or maybe that was all he could drum up anyway.

"Scotty. Scotty."

I leaned over a little toward him to catch it better. "Yes? What is it?" I asked pleasantly.

"I'll give you a hundred thousand dollars. In the bank here in town. Check to bearer. Just let me get over to the desk—write it. Over there, Scotty—other side of the room. Or bring the blank check and pen over here to the bed; I'll write it right where I am. I'll put my arms up high, against the back of the bed; won't move while you're over there getting it."

I considered it, to torture him a little.

"Hundred and fifty thousand, Scotty. The works; everything I've got in my account down here."

"I want Eve back."

His hands were all over me, playing tag, chasing one another all around my shoulders and face.

"Two hundred thousand. Chicago account thrown in. Two hundred and fifty. Listen, won't you listen? A quarter of a million."

"Keep your hands down. You're annoying me. I want Eve. Didn't you hear me? I want Eve."

He rolled his head from side to side on the pillow in despair. "Scotty, everything I've got. New York, Philly. Dummy accounts, safety boxes. Three quarters of a million dollars cash. Everything. You'll own the world. Just let me walk out of here. Just let me walk down the road, the way I am. Just let me be—alive."

"Eve. I want to hear her talk to me again. I want to see her look at me again. I want to see her move around in front of me again."

I'd seen these old-time big shots of the twenties die in movies lots of times, and they always went down spunky, shooting and snarling, "Come and get me." He didn't; he died all spongy. But maybe he was old by now; I don't know. The twenties were way behind us. What do you think he was doing? He was stroking my arm, trying to *wheedle* me into letting him live. Down, and down, and down, like an angry cat's fur.

"Everything, everything—just let me live."

"But I don't want everything. I don't want anything. All I want is something much easier than that. It's hard to rake three quarters of a million dollars together; it takes you all your life; it's hard to hand it over to a stranger just like that! All I want is just Eve. Just arrange to have her brought back to me; that's all you've got to do. That should be easy for a guy like you, used to pulling wires."

"I can't, Scotty," he whimpered.

The low-voiced conversation was nearing the explosion point. I could feel it coming on, though I didn't know from one moment to the other what we were going to say next.

"You're asking me for the one thing I can't do. Why won't you take something else?"

"Then why do you have things done when you can't undo them? Why do you take things away when you can't give them back?"

There it came now. I could feel it pouring down the veins of my arms like a hot tide.

"So the only thing I'll take from you is the one thing I can't give you back: your life."

I plowed deep into him with both arms. I twisted the thing around two ways at once, the thing that was his neck; one hand working one way, the other going against it. It seemed to be in layers; the outer layer, the skin, moved one way; the under part, the muscular column below, went against it. All that came out was a squeak. The echo of a smothered scream that was trapped below as it closed up.

Then you couldn't hear anything much, except the continuous rustling sound the sheets made, as if he were being very restless in his bed. From this side to that, from that side to this. Then his legs would go straight up and pull everything up to a point for a minute, making a tent of the bedclothes. Then they'd collapse again, and the tent would deflate. Then from this side to that, from that side to this, like the blades of a pair of crazed scissors. Then straight up again, almost as if he were practicing calisthenics. It wasn't at that end he was trying to escape; it was at the other, but it couldn't show itself at the other, so it ran down to that end.

I was conscious of everything in the second or two that it was going on. I could even think objectively. I can even remember some of my thoughts. "How long it takes to kill a human being. You never get through." "Isn't he ever going to die? *Die,* will you? *Die,* will you? *Die!*" And with each "*Die*" I'd lunge downward with all might and main, until seams of the woodwork would creak a little, complainingly. And at each lunge his tongue would start forward, as if working on a reverse principle to my pressure. Then it would slip back again. It was like working some kid's toy or plaything, built to do a certain thing when you push in at just the right hidden spot.

I could even see the shadow of my own head, thrown up on the wall by that halo from the lamp. I could see it jitter a little, and then go down out of sight, and then come up again, and then jitter some more. You couldn't make out what it was doing—on the wall. It looked like the head of a man engaged in some strenuous but harmless thing, like packing a crammed valise on top of the bed.

Then suddenly it was swept way offside somewhere, snatched from close before me, and set down again on some far wall, and at different density, as if the original limited halo it had been swimming in had been flushed completely off there and swept away on some new torrential source of reflection. There was a full-length shadow of a man in its place now. Triangular, starting narrow, ending wide, and going all the way up. And I hadn't moved, and the lamp shade hadn't moved, so I knew what it was.

"Wait a minute, Ed—I'll get him!"

The rattles had finally sounded, and the fangs were out.

I swung the two of us around: over, and off the side, and down to the floor in a barrellike somersault. The blast came just as it was half completed. We must have been still above the bed line, in process of going over. It was just dimly noted background noise, an accompaniment to the main event of clawing and flopping that was going on.

When we started I was on top, he was below me; when we ended he was on top, I was below. My hands were still fused to that throat of his; I'd never let go, even falling.

He came down on top of me, heavy and paunchy and bouncy, and then we both just lay there, still.

I didn't feel anything, so I knew it had missed. I knew he was coming over to see.

I saw that I'd killed Roman by now, anyway; he wasn't moving any more. His chest was pasted flat against mine, heart to heart, and I could go by that. There was no counterpoint to my own ticking; I would have felt it if there was any, after such a struggle. So I knew his heart had stopped; he was dead.

Good. That was what I'd been trying for.

He was on his way over to see. We were on the window side of the bed, the two of us, and it was in the way; he couldn't see us from where he was. We both lay still, Roman because he was dead, I because that would bring Jordan over to see. I could see him from under it, his feet in those straw sandals he always wore. I saw them start to move forward, a step at a time. It was funny to see just detached feet, by themselves, walk like that.

I let go the throat. There was nothing to choke out of it any more. The skin almost seemed to stick to my fingers, like pully taffy, I'd been kneading it so long. I got hold of Roman's limp arm in the gaudy striped sleeve, collared it just below the elbow, pushed it up perpendicular above the bed line. My grip around the bone held it up straight, although the hand bent down on itself a little. I let it sort of grab at the coverings atop the bed and stay like that for a minute.

I hoped it looked like a guy who was out of breath and all in trying to lift himself up off the floor by grabbing at something to raise himself against.

It worked. He spoke to the dead hand. He said, "Are you all right, Ed? Did I get him, Ed?"

I spaded the back of my own hand in flat behind the wire from the lamp that ran down beside the wall, close to where my head was resting. Just as his feet were ready to come out past the lower corner of the bed I jerked my wrist out. The lamp came down and went out with a pop and a hiss of glass.

It didn't hurt the rest of the room much; he had the door wide open, but it made it dim and shady down there in that little lane where we were both lying.

He made the turn around the foot of the bed and stopped and looked. I think he could see the pajama stripes across Roman's back even in the half-light. They were uppermost.

He couldn't shoot. There was too much of Roman and not enough of me. He started to lean over, to try to find out what was keeping his boss down like that. That was his mistake. That was just what I wanted him to do.

I grabbed for his ankles, one hand for each. I got them and I jerked. The gun went off again, but in a sort of loose, unguided way. You could tell it was already half out of his hand when the finger guard pulled home. I saw the trajectory of light it spit go upward, on a slant toward the ceiling, instead of downward toward me.

It hit the floor before he did. His arc of descent was wider. It made a neat little rap; he made a heavy sprawling thud.

I wasted a minute to grab for it. Then I skated it deep under the bed, with the curve of my hand for a hocky stick. I didn't want it. I had a funny kind of heat on. I wanted to get at him with my hands.

I tipped Roman, like the dead weight of a mattress lying on you, and pulled myself out from under. He was up again by that time himself. We killed the distance between us with a double-headed rush, came up flat together. We went at each other in the old kind of a fight, the basic kind. Doing your own work yourself.

I would have thought he was no good without his gun, but he was all right. I guess he'd had to fight this way in his green days, before he'd ever had a gun, and it wasn't new to him. My head would jar, and I'd feel it go all the way down my spine and die out, so I knew he'd hit. But that was the only way I knew. I had that sort of frozen-up feeling as much as ever. I was as dead to pain as I was to reason. Maybe it helped; I don't know.

One of mine broke him away from me, sent him all the way back to where the window line ended the room. But they were all open, and he hit one of the open places and went through without interference and kept going out onto the terrace beyond. I went out after him, and it went ahead out there.

My arms were tired and I couldn't feel anything any

more when they hit him, but he'd jar back away from me and my shoulder would sort of recoil; that's how I knew when I had.

One time he went back up against the balustrade I'd climbed over before and bent a little too far out from the waist up. Then recovered and pulled himself forward again. But that made his timing go haywire; he went right into my arm head-on. Added his own momentum to that of the punch, so that he was coming forward to *meet* it, instead of just standing still. It was a bombshell.

My shoulder wrenched itself almost out of gear, and I could see his face going back away from me. It was the last time I saw it. It looked all dopey from the blows; just round and doughy, with the features all tucked in small behind it. What did I care about what his face looked like, anyway? It went back into the night. And then *went out,* in front of my punch-blurred eyes.

I missed the rest of it. He wasn't up there with me any more. I knew he'd gone over. Just one straw sandal had stayed behind.

I looked, and he was already down there. The fall wasn't enough to kill him, and there was a lawn there where he was lying. The dog was at a taut half crouch and bristling; I could see that from where I was.

I don't know if there was blood on Jordan, and that was what did it, or his senses detected the heat of the fight still reeking up from him, and that excited him.

I hollered down, "Get him, Wolf!" I didn't think he would. He was Job's dog, not mine.

His head flattened; his ears lay back, and he went in for his throat like a streak.

The arms and legs came together, like when an insect's helpless on its back, and then opened out again. The dog was busy there in the middle of them.

I turned and went back into the room. I walked zigzag along a straight line back to the bed. The freeze was beginning to thaw, and I felt all mushy.

I turned Roman over with my foot. It was too much trouble to bend down. Something blinked at me in the shadowy light, and for a minute I thought one of his eyes was open again and he was shamming.

Then I saw I hadn't killed him after all. It was just in

front of his ear, a little too far over to be one of his regular eyes. It glistened sleekly, as though somebody'd smudged him there with a dab of wet tar. His own bodyguard had done the job for me.

I couldn't make it out the way I'd come in any more. I went slowly out of the room, leaving the door open behind me, the way Jordan had stood it, and down the upper hall and around to face the stairs.

It was lit up down there now. Job was standing down there in the lower hall at the foot of the stairs. His face was tilted toward me in a static sort of way, as though he'd been standing there motionless like that for some time past.

I looked down at him. "Go ahead," I said dully. "What are you waiting for?"

He just kept looking at me. He didn't say a word until I got all the way down to him.

Then his head hitched curtly toward the end of the hall, where you went out. "I'll unlock the door for you. Go 'head, man. Then I've got to go up and find them and do some phoning in, I reckon."

I passed close by him, eye to eye. "Don't forget to tell them what I look like," I said gruffly.

"I ain't seen no one to tell them about," he said. "They been rowing with each other up there ever since they first come home; I knew it was going to end up like this."

He opened the door for me. Then he said, "She was a lovely lady. I heard them talking about it today; that's how I know."

I went on out into the dark. I looked back at him over my shoulder. "You won't hear them talking about it any more."

He closed the door.

I went around by the side of the house and headed down toward the beach. The dog saw me and left Jordan and came trotting up and fell in beside me. His muzzle was all wet and clotted; he seemed to have grown a stringy beard.

"It was my job," I said, "not yours."

I skirted where Jordan was lying. It was just as well it was dark. It wasn't good to look at him very close any more.

I found the low place in the wall, where it ran down across the sand and into the water; the wall that hadn't been good enough to keep death out. I gave the dog a thump on the ribs, and I hoisted myself up and over.

I could hear the dog running back and forth on the other side, looking for a way to get through so he could come with me. He whined a little.

I didn't blame him. I wouldn't have wanted to stay behind in there either, with just two dead men for company.

CHAPTER XV

MORRO CASTLE WAS LIKE a stubby chunk of pink chalk standing on end in the early-morning light. We drifted in slow past it, so slow we hardly seemed to move at all. But it finally worked its way around behind us, and we were in the harbor, and there was Havana back again. After a night that felt as though it hadn't happened at all.

I came off the ferry and passed through the customs. It was the second time in three days. The guys just looked at me.

"That was just a quick business trip there and back," I explained. "Something that had to be attended to personally."

They thumbed me through.

The sun was low yet, and the roof tops were only beginning to get their first coat of it; the dazzling paint job hadn't been laid on heavy. Down on the sidewalks it was still cool and shady.

I was beginning to know my way around Havana. I knew where I wanted to go, and that always helps. I headed straight for police headquarters and Acosta's office. But I walked slow; I took my time. It was early yet, and I wanted to give him time to get there.

He was. I found him at his desk by the time I got in. He must have just got there ahead of me. He was starting to straighten up things from the day before. He looked up when he saw me standing there in the door.

"What brings you around here so early?" he exclaimed.

I came the rest of the way in and closed the door after me.

"I've just killed two men in Miami, Florida," I said.

His hands stopped fussing with the papers, fell sort of flat and quiet on top of them, but without letting them go.

He took a minute's time to look down. Then he looked up at me. He looked at me a long time.

"Why do you come in here?" he said in a low voice that I could hardly hear. "Why didn't you go to *them*, up there?"

"I don't know," I admitted with a sort of half-baked smile. "I guess because—it's closer to her, down here. Or maybe because a guy likes to go to a guy that's already somewhat familiar to him, about a thing like that. That he's already spoken to and knows; who isn't a stranger." I laughed at it myself.

He quit looking at me finally, started shoving a lot of papers around. As though something or other was over, and he was about ready for the next thing.

I waited as long as I could. Finally I got tired. "Well, what are you going to do?"

"About what?"

"About what I told you when I came in here."

He got annoyed, like a busy man does when you pester him about something. His forehead pleated up impatiently. "I don't speak English so good," he snapped. "I often miss hearing things that are said to me, especially when they're said too fast."

"I can say it slower. I just killed two men in Miami. Eddie Roman and Bruno Giordano or Jordan. Is that slow enough?"

He shook his head. "My English stinks today. If I should get a radiogram from the Miami police telling me to hold a man named Scott for murder up there, that would be different. Then I'd go out looking for a man named Scott, and when I found him I'd hold him for them. I'd have to. Unless or until that should happen, would you mind not coming in here and mumbling things in English that I don't quite catch?"

"Suppose you never hear from them?" I said. "It's quite likely that you won't."

"Then how can I know about a thing unless I'm properly notified?" he flared. "I'm not a mind reader, you know!

Now, *mira,* you been standing around here ten minutes, and I still don't know what you want. I'm a busy man. *Buenos días, señor.* There's a door right behind you."

It finally sank in, what he was trying to do. I suppose I should have thanked him. I wasn't sure it was worth it. What was he giving me? A long-term option on a headache, instead of a quick cure. I wasn't sure he had any thanks coming.

I turned and drifted toward the door he'd pointed out. "I'll be around the town," I said.

"I know," I heard him murmur. "Stick to rum. It goes quicker."

A cop came in all flustered and jabbered something to him a mile a minute. He was holding the back of his hand with a handkerchief, as though it had been scratched or bitten.

Acosta threw up his hands and raked them through his hair. He turned to me suddenly. "How much money you got on you?"

I told him.

He didn't seem to care how much it was. "Would you mind putting it up as bail, so we can get that—that epidemic off our hands?"

I didn't know what he meant for a minute.

"That girl, that woman! She's been raising Cain in there all night, all day yesterday. If you haven't got enough, I'll pay it out of my own pocket. Anything to get her out of here!"

I handed it over to him. "What are you holding her for, anyway? Material witness? She doesn't—"

"She lifted the pocket watch of one of my detectives right as they were bringing her in in custody the first time. Somebody that didn't know any better let the charge go down on the blotter, and we've been stuck with her ever since! It's worse than one of these hurricanes that blows in from the sea every now and then; at least they go right on out again."

I kept my face straight with difficulty. "She must be slipping," I felt like saying. "What was she doing with her other hand at the time?"

The fine or whatever it was went through, and in a minute or two you could hear a scuffling and commotion coming down the corridor from in back somewhere. You could hear it long before it got there. As though a heavy trunk were being bounced around, or as though the trunk were bouncing its handlers around. Either way.

Then the door slapped open. It was taking two of them to hold her. And even then they could have used a couple extra pairs of hands apiece. She was keeping them busy.

"Release her, release her." Acosta waved at them hectically. "If I have any more of my men bitten I'll have them all at the dispensary. Open the street door," he added prudently.

They took their hands off her quick, like they were only too glad to. They even stepped noticeably back, gave her plenty of room.

She didn't take immediate advantage of the invitingly open outside door. First she looked down at herself. She brushed off all the places where their hands had been. She made the pantomime eloquent, wringing out her hands separately as though she were dropping off clotted filth. Then she readjusted her attire by giving it a half turn around on her here and there. Like armor that had slipped its moorings.

Then she started *in* toward him, instead of out the other way. She came on slow and sultry. She had on her war walk. She was carrying that chip on her hip again, like the other night in the room when I'd first met her. She looked tough as gravel. She looked dangerous to monkey with or get in the way of.

Acosta stood his ground—or rather sat it out, behind the desk. There were two of his own men present, and he couldn't do otherwise. But if I read the expression on his face correctly, he would have given anything to shift back a little farther, chair and all.

She came to a halt about halfway over to the desk, sent him a glare that should have charred him where he sat.

Everybody was noticeably quiet; himself and the two cops over by the door as well. After all, men are instinctively peaceloving animals. Particularly when they're liable to get badly mauled for not being.

I cleared my throat to see if I could draw her off. She hadn't looked at me at all. "Hello, Midnight," I said deprecatingly. It didn't work. She kept her eyes on him. "I'll talk to you outside," she said. "I don't like the air in this place."

Then she swung with one side of her mouth. One of the documents in front of him on the desk jumped a little.

Then she turned and went on back, walking slow and sultry, dangerous to tamper with. The two cops at the door shifted even farther aside, gave her all the clearance she needed.

She stood there in the open doorway for a minute, broadside to all of us, facing the way out. She gave him a final searing glare by way of postscript. Then she flexed one knee joint, brought up something, put a carefully preserved cigar segment to her mouth. And then as a final index of her regard for these surroundings she reached up toward the top of the door, struck a great transverse swipe all the way down across it that ended in a sizzling match flare. A moment later the steaming matchstick landed across the threshold, well inside the room, in the general direction of Acosta.

She moved on, passed from view. A little cigar smoke came drifting back past the vacant doorway.

I looked at Acosta. He was surreptitiously mopping his brow and trying to pretend that he wasn't. Then he took a blotter and touched it lightly to the document that had jumped before. "Close that door," he barked. "I don't want her back in here again."

I caught up with her outside on the street a couple of moments later. She was walking along slow, taking her time, not afraid of anyone, cop or civilian, making them get out of her way. I called to her and went chasing after her.

"Well, it's over, Midnight," I said, falling into step beside her.

"It's over, *guapo,*" she agreed.

There didn't seem to be anything more to say about it, so we didn't say it.

We walked over in the general direction of Sloppy's. We stopped when we got to the corner below.

"I'd like to ask you in for a drink," I said, "but—"

"I know. There's someone waiting for you in there. Flowers on a grave."

She dusted off my sleeve with a comradely flick of her hand, and that was our way of saying good-by, I guess.

Two ships that pass in the night; two paths that cross in the dark.

I watched her for a moment, then I turned. She went her way, and I went in.

I stood there with a daiquiri, right where we'd stood that night. Her dying words came back to me. "Let me know how that picture we took together turns out."

"It turned out okay, darling," I said softly. "It turned out okay." I held up my glass to her, wherever she was. Then I snapped it against the bar.

It was lonely standing there by myself at the bar like that.